Also by Anchee Min:

Red Azalea
Katherine
Becoming Madame Mao

WILD
GINGER
ANCHEE
MIN

Published in Great Britain by The Women's Press Ltd, 2002
A member of the Namara Group
34 Great Sutton Street, London EC1V 0LQ
www.the-womens-press.com

First published in USA by Houghton Mifflin, 2002

British Library Cataloguing-in-Publication Data
A catalogue record for this book is available from the British
Library.

ISBN 0 7043 4746 6

Printed and bound in Great Britain by Creative Print
Design Wales, Ebbw Vale

During a certain period of our lives, we possess youth.
The rest we spend living in the memories of it.

—from the diary of a former Red Guard

1

In my memory she has a pair of foreign-colored eyes, the pupils yellow with a hint of green. They reminded me of a wildcat. She stood by the classroom door, her face in shadow. Behind her the sun looked like a giant red lantern. As the sun rose, suddenly the light spilled out. The beam hit the windows, bounced, and was reflected in her eyes. It was there, in her eyes, that I saw water in motion, the bottom of a pond clearly illuminated by the light. The water weeds swayed gracefully like ancient long-sleeve dancers.

I remember my thought: she's not Chinese. Then I thought no, it's impossible. It must be the sunlight playing tricks on me. She was just like me, a girl with thick short braids at the side of her ears. She was in a blue Mao jacket. Her right hand held an abacus. She wore an old pair of army shoes with her big toes on their way out. No Red Guard armband on her left arm. I remember my fear from that instant. It was what connected us — a sign of political uncertainty. I thought of Hot Pepper, the bully girl, the head of the Red Guard. She would definitely suspect that the newcomer was a reactionary.

I remember I began to feel sorry for the newcomer. The same way I felt for myself. I was rejected for membership in the Red Guard because I was not from a three-generation-of-labor family. My parents and grandparents were teachers. It didn't matter that we were just as poor. We lived in a converted garage in Shanghai. Eight people in one room.

Hot Pepper believed in violence. Hitting was part of her treatment. She said that she had to "pump" the "dirty bourgeois blood" out of me. The authorities and society encouraged her. People of my category were considered to have "reactionary dust" in our thoughts. It was Mao's teaching that "the dust won't go away unless there is a broom." Hot Pepper called herself a "revolutionary broom."

Hot Pepper had a pair of mice eyes and an otterlike body. No neck. Her bangs were so long that her eyes looked as if they were behind bars. She wore a Red Guard armband and an extra-large green military uniform. She was very proud of her uniform because it had four pockets. Pockets were an indication of rank — the more pockets, the higher the rank. The uniform was from her uncle, who had served in the People's Liberation Army. Hot Pepper also wore two palm-size ceramic Mao buttons, which were pinned on each side of her chest. The buttons were peach-colored morning sky with a tiny Mao head in the middle. From a distance they looked like two breasts with Mao heads as nipples.

Every morning Hot Pepper led a team to block the school gate. They were there to examine everyone's loyalty toward Chairman Mao. The school's requirement was that everyone bring the "three-piece treasure": a Mao button, a *Little Red Book* (Mao quotations), and, if you were a Red Guard, an armband. If you forgot, Hot Pepper lined you up and held you until the bell rang. Sometimes Hot Pepper picked people at random to quiz them on Mao quotations. She would say the page number and the person was expected to recite the quotation. If the person made a mistake, Hot Pepper would decide on a form of punishment. She would either order him to stand by the gate and read the quotation aloud one hundred times until he was able to recite it, or she would order him to clean the school's restrooms for a week.

Every morning when I got near the gate and saw Hot Pepper's shadow, my heart would pound. I could feel my fingers turning cold and my breath shorten. I made sure I brought all three pieces and updated all my Mao quotations. Still, Hot Pepper found fault every time. She would say that I hadn't made the proper pause at a comma or at the period. When I did pause she would say that I recited the paragraph too slowly, that I was trying to cheat.

I was excluded from school activities, including my favorite sports, table tennis and swimming. It didn't matter that I was a good swimmer. Hot Pepper believed that

I would betray the country and swim across the ocean. "She'll swim as fast as she can, out of the sea, into the Pacific Ocean, where a Western ship will be waiting. She will be picked up and sell all our national secrets to the enemy."

It was 1969, the midst of the great movement called the Cultural Revolution. I was fourteen years old and attended the July First Elementary School. July 1 was the birthday of the Communist party. I wasn't learning much in those years. The Cultural Revolution had started when I was seven. We had been studying Mao. We were taught to write our teacher's name on the ground with brushes and cross the characters with black ink. We were on the streets parading all the time. We celebrated Chairman Mao's every new teaching, copying his words onto big posters. Fifty-six of us in the class. Fifty-six posters. We put up the posters on doors and gates around the neighborhood. It was our mission in life. As a line leader, Hot Pepper always carried an electric loudspeaker while I, as a line tail, carried the heavy paste bucket and wet broom.

Once in a while we were shoved back into the classroom. We were taught basic math in the mornings. In the afternoons, on odd-numbered days, a guest speaker who had horrible stories about the old society would be invited from the countryside or a factory. The entire three-hour speeches demonstrated one thing: without Chairman Mao we would all be dead. It was effective. We all began to believe firmly that we were saved and protected by Chairman Mao. We began to love him. On even-numbered days, we

4

would be assigned to read heroic stories about soldiers who died defending the country and honoring Chairman Mao.

My biggest wish was to be old enough to join the People's Liberation Army. I couldn't wait to die in order to prove my loyalty to Mao. I wanted to go to Vietnam, North Korea, or Albania. I wanted to fight the enemies like those heroes whose stories I had been reading.

My mother said that people had too much fire in their bodies. When I asked why, she lowered her voice and said it was because the Communist party had banned the worship of the spirits. And this was how our ancestors showed their anger. Right after hearing my mother's words, I started my menstrual cycle. I had no idea what it was. I thought the fire my mother had described had boiled down into my body.

Since turning twelve I had been feeling uncomfortable with my body. I was ashamed of my developing chest. It was terrifying. I wrapped my chest with three layers of cloth plus a tight undershirt. Even in the summer heat I wore the same shirt, ignoring the skin rashes. I wondered how other girls were coping. Most of them began to act hunchbacked. Some girls were proud of themselves because their chests were as flat as washboards. One day a dozen girls from the neighboring class sobbed together. It was because boys had threatened to "marry" them.

We were again learning nothing else except Mao's teachings on how to carry on the Cultural Revolution. "The battle between the bourgeoisie class and the proletarian class has intensified and is taking the most violent forms." Violence was a part of living then. People divided themselves into factions according to their backgrounds, and each faction tried to prove itself Mao's loyalists. Hot Pepper was proud because she was born "red." She came from a family of illiterate miners. Even though I didn't necessarily belong in the anti-Maoist category, I was told that I had to earn my right to breathe. "When I order a reactionary to crawl, you crawl," said Hot Pepper, "or my umbrella will teach you a lesson."

"Class! We have a new person here," Mrs. Cheng, our teacher, a woman in her late twenties, announced. Her voice carried a cautious tone. I noticed that she didn't say "a new comrade" or "a classmate." She said "a person." That was another sign. It gave obscurity to the girl's background. "She is a transferring student from Number Nineteen District. Her name is Wild Ginger, pronounced as Wu-Jiang Pei."

"Wild Ginger?" Hot Pepper's eyebrows frowned. "What a strange name!" She began to laugh shrilly. "How do you write it?" The sound was characteristic of the bully. It gave me goose bumps every time.

"*Wu* as 'Wild,' a luxuriant growth of weeds. It is written with a Grass head on top of the character Nothingness," the newcomer said, stepping out of the sun's shadow. There was no fear in her voice. "*Jiang* as 'Ginger' with a flat tone. You can call me Wild Ginger."

6

The class was quiet, actually surprised.

Hot Pepper stood up. "But Wu-Jiang can also be described as 'A wasteland.' Correct me if I'm wrong, Mrs. Cheng."

Mrs. Cheng pretended to be deaf.

The girl raised her eyes cautiously.

I blinked in disbelief: the sunlight hadn't fooled me. The pupils were yellow-green! I stared. Is she a foreigner? The eyes were almond shaped, wide apart; they couldn't have been more Oriental. The nose had a high bridge, narrow and long, with only a short distance between her nose and upper lip. The shape of her face was like a goose egg, and her neck was gracefully long. Her skin color was lighter then everyone else's in the room. Except for her gleaming black-lacquer hair, she could indeed be taken for a foreigner.

"What's wrong with your eyes? Is it a kind of disease?" Hot Pepper sat back down and kicked off her shoes.

The girl made no reply, but brushed a strand of hair behind her ear.

Hot Pepper continued, "This is definitely not a pair of proletarian's eyes. Red Guards, be prepared to perform your duty."

The class watched in silence.

My worry for the newcomer increased. Not long ago Hot Pepper had done this to me. It was my first day too. Hot Pepper wouldn't let me into the classroom. She questioned why I was wearing a boy's jacket with buttons on the right side instead of the left. I explained that my family had no money to buy clothes so I wore my cousin's hand-me-downs. Hot Pepper laughed and told everyone that she had found lice in my hair.

People in the class were afraid to stand up to Hot Pepper. Fear not only tamed them but made them her accomplices. Often, after Hot Pepper beat someone, that person turned to join Hot Pepper's gang. Hot Pepper said that she had learned her way from her uncle, who was a horse trainer in the army. "The technique is called *xia-ma-wei*. It is a warning against insubordination. My uncle once showed me how it was done with an unruly horse. It was really simple. He gave a head-on blow at the first encounter. He beat the shit out of the animal!"

"My name is Wild Ginger." The sound was uncompromising. The girl looked straight at Hot Pepper. An excitement stirred inside me. Finally! Someone was standing up to the untouchable bully! I only wondered how long she would last.

Wild Ginger looked determined. She tilted her chin high when she spoke.

"Your name doesn't sound proletarian enough," Hot Pepper sneered. "Change it! How about Supporter-of-Red?"

"No, thank you."

"Then you are not coming into the class."

"I am not changing my name."

"Are you an anti-Maoist?"

"I am Wild Ginger."

"State your background! Is there an enemy in your family?"

"Who are you to ask me this?"

"I can tell right away that you have an evil background from your appearance. You have a very reactionary look."

"Mind your own business, please."

"Explain why your pupils are such a strange color!"

The girl paused for a second. "Well, may I ask why you have a short neck? Show me your neck and I will tell you about my pupils."

The class laughed.

An earsplitting sound came from the loudspeaker hung from the ceiling. "Ceremony!" the party secretary's voice from the speaker yelled.

"Ceremony!" Mrs. Cheng echoed. She was rather relieved by the interruption. "The Mao Quotation Book on the table. Hurry up, everyone!"

To the music of "The Red in the East," the class rose.

Mrs. Cheng quickly took Wild Ginger to a vacant bench in the front row on my right. It was the worst seat. She had to look sideways in order to see what was written on the board. Wild Ginger placed her school bag inside the desk drawer and took out her Mao Quotation Book.

We began to sing "The Red in the East," the slow and clumsy song that had replaced the national anthem. It was originally shouted out by a peasant in mid-China. I noticed that Mrs. Cheng's chest was wet again. She stood with her milk seeping. Two round spots. The circles grew bigger and bigger. Her bra underneath the blouse was soaked and was clearly visible. She had been to the restroom but it didn't help. She was not allowed to go home to her newborn.

Hot Pepper strode from her seat to the front of the class to lead the recitation of quotations. We chanted mindlessly. It would usually last two hours.

Bored, I stole a glance at Wild Ginger. From where I sat, I saw her profile. She had amazingly long, thick eyelashes. Her sleeves had worn edges and her navy blue pants were so worn and washed out that her knees showed. She sat with her hands constantly scratching her limbs as if she had a skin disease. Her mouth wasn't moving in sync with the rest of the class. After a while she bent down toward the desk drawer and fumbled with her bag. She dug out Mao's book and flipped through the pages. Obviously she hadn't been following our reading — she was unable to locate the page we were on.

We were reciting Mao's *Three Famous Essays* — "Serve the People," "In Memory of Norman Bethune," and "The Foolish Man Who Moved the Mountain." I could tell Wild Ginger was faking. It surprised me that she was not a bit nervous. She turned the pages back and forth. Her nails were dirty. The hands were covered with frostbite.

"'When one dies for the people, his worth weighs heavier than a mountain,'" the recitation continued. Hot Pepper's eyes brushed across the room. "'When one dies of

any other cause, the weight is lighter than a feather . . .'"
I felt sleepy but reminded myself of an incident during which a boy was expelled from the school because he couldn't stay awake during Mao readings.

"'. . . Although we come from different backgrounds, we are fighting for one purpose. It is to liberate the world, to provide the poor with food and shelter. We are the true revolutionaries. We live like a big family where everyone is treated as a brother or sister. We are learning to be truthful, kind, and caring . . .'"

I looked at the Mao portrait on the wall. The Chairman had kind-looking features. Smiling eyes, glowing cheeks, a round nose, and a gentle mouth. It was a peaceful face. Hot Pepper once said that if you stared at Mao's portrait long enough, the Chairman would come alive. His eyes would blink and his lips would open. I experimented with staring, but the man never came alive. I was getting bored looking at him. But there was nothing else besides the portrait on the wall in the classroom. A couple of months ago I scribbled in my notebook during the reciting. Mrs. Cheng stopped me. Later she explained that she was trying to protect me. Although she didn't spell the words out, I understood the message. She was right. If Hot Pepper had caught me, I would have been expelled from the school as a reactionary.

Mrs. Cheng's wet spots had melted into one large blot.
Hot Pepper was enjoying the sound of her own voice. She was showing off her skill by speeding up. We were

reaching the end of the section. My fear of Hot Pepper sank in. I began to think how to escape the beating today. Maybe I should try to walk through the school's back fence instead of the gate. What if people saw me? They would report me to Hot Pepper. No one could stop Hot Pepper, not even Mrs. Cheng.

I often prayed for Hot Pepper to be sick. Her sneeze brought me delight and hope for the day. But she was strong as a spring bear. She often asked others if they could "spare" food. To give or not give her what she had set her eyes on signaled the difference between being a revolutionary and a reactionary. Her mouth smelled like a garbage bin. Her teeth were corn yellow. Her tongue was always black and blue from licking her ink pen. Now she was staring at Mrs. Cheng's chest. She made faces with Titi and Yaya — her gang members. They giggled. The class saw them and some joined in. Suddenly Hot Pepper's expression changed. Her eyes stopped at one spot. Her mouth hung open as if shocked. I turned to see what she was looking at. I was shocked too: Wild Ginger had laid her head down on folded arms. She was sleeping.

Umbrellas fell on my head like storms — my day's meal had begun. Hot Pepper and her gang attacked me from all directions. I tried to protect myself from the blows with my arms. In the meantime I searched for an escape. Hot Pepper came to block my exit. Her umbrella landed on my shoulders. I cried out in pain. Yaya and Titi came and began to punch my chest. Hot Pepper circled behind me. In a swift motion her knees knocked right into my joints. I fell on my kneecaps, my mouth in the grass.

Titi and Yaya clapped. I heard Hot Pepper's laughter.

People passed by me. No one stopped. I had told my mother about Hot Pepper's treatment. Mother had come to the school and had complained to Mrs. Cheng. Mrs. Cheng told my mother that she had gone to the principal and was told that Hot Pepper represented the Red Guards and was permitted by Chairman Mao to do "whatever necessary to change the world." "If your child had come from a working class family she would have been protected."

The beating resumed. My hair was pulled. My sleeves were gone by now. My collar was coming off. I was unable to reach the gate. The more I struggled, the harder they hit. Wrapping my head with my arms my tears flowed in despair. I shouted, "Chairman Mao will hear me now! I am his loyalist too! I have never misspelled one word of his teachings. My test scores are all excellent. You, Hot Pepper, your treatment is unfair and cruel. If Chairman Mao learns what's happening to me he will be upset!"

"Quite the opposite!" Hot Pepper's umbrella chopped down. "He will say, 'Wipe that rat off the face of the earth! If the enemy doesn't surrender, send it to die!'"

Suddenly the umbrellas stopped. There was a cry. Someone had punched Hot Pepper. Under my elbow, I stole a glance. It was the new girl, Wild Ginger. She was wrestling with Hot Pepper. She pulled Hot Pepper's umbrella away from her and smashed it against the concrete. Enraged, Hot Pepper threw herself at Wild Ginger. Her teeth were in Wild Ginger's blouse. The buttons on their jackets began to pop. Suddenly Wild Ginger landed a heavy punch. Hot Pepper fell backward and landed on her butt.

"An enemy has revealed herself!" Hot Pepper shouted. "This is the one who slept through the Mao study section! Look at that funny-looking face! She must carry the blood of a Western opium seller! Comrades, let's go to the secretary's office! Let's dig out her dossier!"

2

"This is exactly what I suspected." Hot Pepper leafed through a pile of files and announced to the class, "Wild Ginger's father, the late Mr. Pei, was French. He was a spy. Although he is dead it doesn't mean that he is free from the crime he caused. Wild Ginger's mother is Chinese, but I am sure she is nothing more than a whore. Wild Ginger is a born spy. Chairman Mao teaches us, 'To the reactionary of all sorts we must be ruthless!'"

Within seconds, Wild Ginger was hit by umbrellas. Soon her cheeks began to swell and her nose bled. Her braids broke loose and her jacket was torn apart. "Give up!" Hot Pepper and the gang shouted. "Surrender! Take us the proletarians as your master or we will beat you to death!"

Wild Ginger rose in blood. Her eyes stared like a mad bull's.

Hot Pepper lunged again, citing Mao. "'Kill the bourgeois bugs! Save the patient! Kill the bourgeois bugs! Save the patient!' May Fourth, 1939, *Selected Works of Mao Tse-tung*. Volume eleven, page two-forty-six, 'The Orientation of the Youth Movement.'"

The gang joined in reciting. "'How should we judge whether a youth is a revolutionary? How can we tell? There can only be one criterion, namely whether or not he is willing to integrate himself with the broad masses of workers and peasants and does so in practice. If he is willing to do so and actually does so, he is a revolutionary; otherwise he is a nonrevolutionary or a counterrevolutionary. If today he integrates himself with the masses of workers and peasants, then today he is the revolutionary; if tomorrow he ceases to do so or turns around to oppress the common people, then he becomes a nonrevolutionary or a counter-revolutionary.'"

Like a cornered animal Wild Ginger used her abacus as a shield; she fought until the abacus fell apart. Throwing away the broken frame she took up her school bag. The gang came to seize her again. I tried to help but got pulled and pinned down by Titi and Yaya. Hot Pepper and her other gang members got Wild Ginger's school bag. All her books and materials flew out. She was punched down to the ground. While the others held her head and feet, Hot Pepper hopped on her back and began to stab with her umbrella.

With ear-piercing cries, Wild Ginger gave in.

Hot Pepper shouted a Mao quotation with a tone of victory: "'Reading is learning, but applying is also learning and the more important kind of learning at that. Our chief method is to learn warfare through warfare. We learn through fighting in war. A revolutionary war is a mass undertaking; it is often not a matter of first learning and then doing, but of doing and then learning, for doing is itself learning."'

Lying on her stomach, Wild Ginger gasped. Hot Pepper and her gang walked away. The campus became quiet. I got up from where I lay.

Wild Ginger rose slowly, crawling to her feet. She looked around for her shoes. The beads of the abacus and the pages of her books were scattered all over. She located a shoe behind the bushes and went to fetch it. She hopped on one leg, in pain, her face torn. On her way back she picked up her school bag. The buckles were gone.

I walked toward Wild Ginger. I picked up the abacus beads and the pages. I wanted to thank her but didn't know how to begin.

"I suppose this is your sleeve?" Wild Ginger picked up a piece of fabric that matched my jacket and passed it to me. "The other one is behind the bushes."

I nodded a thank you and passed her the pages.

"What's your name?" she asked, stuffing the pages into her bag.

"Maple."

"I see. You turn red in fall." She smiled and began to tie her shoelace.

"Are you making fun of my name?"

"No, not at all." She wiped the dripping blood off her mouth. "I like your name. It sounds proletarian, Maoist. It's perfect. Your parents must be very thoughtful people . . . Anyway, how do you write it?"

"The character Wind with a Wood on the left-hand side."

"You are quite like your name." She stood up and patted the dirt off her buttocks. "You bend."

What could I say? What did she know about Hot Pepper? I started to assemble the abacus.

"I didn't say it was your fault, did I?" She was sorting the pages and trying to restore the textbook.

"Anyway, thanks for coming to my rescue."

"You're welcome." As if caught by a sudden twist of pain she got down on her knees.

"Are you all right?"

"I . . . am fine."

"I'm sorry."

"No, don't ever feel sorry for me. I take the wounds as my medals."

What a thought! "Do you fight a lot?"

"With my kind of looks, people don't leave me alone."

"Do you win in the fights?"

"Well, most of the time I lose. Once I almost got my teeth knocked out."

"You are brave."

"I wouldn't put it that way."

"I am sure you . . . you are aware that you do look a little foreign. Is your father really French?"

"Half French. My grandfather is French."

"Where is France? Is it an imperialist country like the U.S.A.?"

"I have no idea. I have never seen a world map. My mother once said that it was in Europe and was a beautiful agricultural country. But how can I trust my mother?"

"So Hot Pepper was right about your dossier?"

"Well, one can't choose one's parents, can one?"

"Of course not."

She made a deep, old-woman-like sigh.

"I'm sorry, Wild Ginger."

"My mother was wrong. She thought that transferring me to another school would help."

"Well, you didn't fight for yourself this time."

"Believe me, it makes no difference. Sooner or later my looks will be everyone's excuse to hit or make fun of me. To tell you the truth, at my old school people were rougher. They beat me with metal belt buckles."

"What are you going to do?"

"I don't know. I can't stop them. Being submissive is not going to do it either, and that I know for sure."

I sighed, thinking about my own situation. Every muscle of my body ached.

"You take it as if you deserve it." She started to walk toward the gate and I followed. "Why don't you fight back, Maple? At least you should show them your disapproval."

"What's the use? In any case I won't win. I am alone."

"Not anymore." Wild Ginger picked up a willow branch and swung it in the air.

I looked at her.

She cracked the branch like a whip. It snapped and made a crispy sound.

A strange warm feeling came through me. My tears gushed up involuntarily.

"Here's your abacus," I managed to say. "Hot Pepper will break it again if she sees you hanging out with me."

"Or you with me." She smiled. "Where do you live?"

"Number 347 Red Heart Road. And you?"

"Not far from you. Stalin Road behind Chia Chia Lane."

"I like your name, by the way."

That night for the first time in a long while I felt at peace. Life was changing its color from dark to light. My despair eased. Wild Ginger filled my mind. I told my mother about my new friend. I described her fearlessness. I didn't mind when Mother fell asleep. She snored before I finished. I kept going. I needed to hear Wild Ginger's name and hear her story.

The late summer night in Shanghai was humid. I could hear my stomach rumble. We were too poor to afford full meals. My family slept on the floor on a bamboo mat. My three sisters and three brothers laid their arms and legs across one another. In sleep they were engaged in a war. They were fighting for food and space. My second brother's toe was in my third sister's mouth. My youngest brother's butt was on my mother's chest. My second sister shouted "Buns! Green onion buns!" and rolled off the mat as if chasing someone who had taken her buns. My oldest brother wiggled his body and stuck his head in between the table leg and the chair. "Buns? Where is the bun?" His hands grabbed my shoulder.

Unable to sleep, I got up. I decided to write a letter to my father, who had been sent to a forced labor collective. I hadn't seen him for almost a year. I told him that I looked forward to school now. Although I still expected beating and assault, the thought that I was no longer alone cheered me.

3

Lists of the names of the "newly discovered enemies" were posted on the neighborhood's bulletin boards. Among them was Mrs. Pei, Wild Ginger's mother. She was accused as a spy and was ordered to attend public meetings to denounce her husband and confess her crime. The neighbors and children were asked by the head of the district to keep their eyes on her and report any sign of resistance.

I ran to Wild Ginger to tell her the news. Her house was in an elegant compound located at the deep end of the lane. It was built during the French colonial period before the Liberation and was the greenest district in the city. The house was half hidden in the shade under a large fig tree. The entrance was run-down but still had an elegant look. It reminded me of an abandoned, aging concubine.

I knocked on the door. It was half open. A limping dog came out. "Come on in," Wild Ginger greeted me. "Maple's here, Mother."

I entered the hallway. It was spacious. Off it were old white rooms with windows on three sides. The leaf-patterned curtains were drawn, making the light inside dim and soft. Lying on an old sofa, Mrs. Pei, a middle-aged, gray-haired woman, welcomed me. She was very thin although still pretty, like an old porcelain goddess. Layers of sheets and blankets covered her from the waist down. In front of her, scattered across the floor, were a variety of potted plants. There were orchids, thick-leaved bamboo, camellias, and red grass.

"Mrs. Pei," I said politely.

She made an effort to sit up, but her strength failed her. She lay back down and gasped, "Excuse me." She looked nervous. "Water, Ginger. Come on in, Maple dear. Has anyone seen you coming to the house?"

"No. I hid behind the fig tree for a long time before I knocked at your door. I made sure no one saw me."

Mrs. Pei sighed with relief.

"Have you seen the bulletin?" Wild Ginger asked me.

"That's why I'm here, to tell you about it. It's on everybody's door."

"The neighborhood activists posted them this morning." Her voice was strangely distant and matter-of-fact.

"What . . . are you going to do?" I turned to look at Mrs. Pei.

Mrs. Pei said nothing. She stared at the ceiling.

"Does Mother have a choice?" Wild Ginger poured me a cup of water. "She made the mistake of marrying a foreigner. She has to live with the consequences. She knew that. But it's not fair to me. I am the victim. I am the casualty of her battle. But, Maple, let me tell you, that marriage was not a crime, it was a mistake. A human error."

"It was not a mistake." Mrs. Pei pushed herself to rise. "Nor an error. He is your father!"

"Mother, enough. I hate that man."

"How dare you disrespect your father! You daughter of no piety!" Mrs. Pei groaned.

"I hate that very thought."

"You carry his blood."

"I am disgusted."

"You don't know who he was."

"He was a spy."

"He was not."

"Why did he come to China? What business did a foreigner have to do with China?"

"He loved China. He was a diplomat. It was his job. He wanted to help China thrive."

"No. He was a spy. Spying was his job. He was sent by the Western imperialists. Helping China thrive was his disguise. It was false. Helping the Western imperialists to exploit China was the truth. You were too blind to see it. You were foolish."

"You bastard!"

"The sound of truth hurts your ears, doesn't it?"

"How could you trust what the authorities tell you?"

"I trust Chairman Mao's representatives! I trust Chairman Mao!"

"You've been brainwashed!"

"Watch out, Mother! You are sounding dangerous!"

"I am your mother. I'll risk my life to tell you the truth!"

"You are a pitiful victim."

"Shut up!"

"I pity you, Mother. I truly do. And I pity myself too, although I don't want to."

"Don't listen to her, Maple . . ." Mrs. Pei fell back to the sofa. Closing her eyes she breathed with difficulty. Her chest was rising and falling. "Ginger is mad, like the rest of China."

"I am not mad, but you definitely are, Mother! You have been living in a dream created by that Frenchman, and worse, you refuse to wake up."

"Ginger!"

"Wake up, Mother!"

"Ginger! I should have listened to my great-aunt! I should have given you the name she had suggested, 'Plain Water.' It was to calm you and tame your character. Oh, how I rejected and upset her! She hired a fortuneteller who told us that there was too much fire in you when you were born. I was told that you would burn yourself into a wasteland. But I didn't care. I liked the passion that fire signified! Your father and I named you Wu-Jiang, 'Wild Ginger,' because we loved the fire in you! We thought that it was special. Your father treasured the wildness. We hoped that you would grow up to be as free as you want to be. But how could I have known it would turn out like this! What a retribution! . . . Maple, Ginger's father loved China and he loved his daughter. He died of cancer when she was five. He was a noble man."

"Chairman Mao teaches us" — the daughter interrupted the mother — "'It is impossible for one class member to love the member of his opposite class.'"

"You were your father's everything!"

"I don't want to hear it."

"How can you have the heart to do this?"

"You are insulting me, Mother."

"For God's sake!"

"The hell with God the ghost-head!"

"You'll be punished for scorning the Lord."

"To be born of such parents is to be punished. I have been serving my sentence. I have been called a little spy in every school I attended, and I have been treated with distrust from both authorities and classmates. No matter how hard I've tried, no one has accepted me. Look!" She pulled up her sleeves and revealed bruises.

Suddenly I understood her habit of scratching. It was not a skin disease but the healing of her bruises that made her itch.

"Don't make me say words that will hurt you, Mother," Wild Ginger continued. "All I want in life is to be able to be accepted and trusted, to be a Maoist like everyone else in this country. This is not too much to ask, is it? Is it, Mother? But because of you and that Frenchman, I am doomed."

"Help me, God." Mrs. Pei buried her face in the pillow.

"Sure, help me, God, the devil is taking my child," Wild Ginger said hysterically. "Mother, don't force me to make a report on you. Outcast and rejected as I am, I will denounce you and move myself out of this stinky house!"

Mrs. Pei began to shiver under the sheets. After a few deep breaths she said, weeping, "Jean-Michel, take me, please. For I can bear no more . . ."

What the daughter expressed here didn't make sense to the mother, but it made perfect sense to me. To become a Maoist for our generation was like attaining the state of Nirvana for a Buddhist. We might not yet understand the literature of Maoism, but since kindergarten we were taught that the process, the conversion — to enslave our body and soul, to sacrifice what was requested in order to "get there" — was itself the meaning of our lives. The sacrifice meant learning not only to separate ourselves from, but to actually denounce, those we loved most when judgment called. We were also taught to manage the pain that came with such actions. It was called the "true tests." The notion was so powerful that youths throughout the nation became caught up in it. From 1965 to 1969 millions of young people stood out despite their pain and publicly denounced their family members, teachers, and mentors in order to show devotion toward Mao. They were honored.

I understood the importance of being a Maoist. I myself tried desperately to survive the "true tests." I must say that we were not blind in believing in Chairman Mao Tse-tung.

Worshiping him as the savior of China was not crazy. The truth was that without him leading the Communist party and its armies, China would be a sliced melon, swallowed up long ago by foreign powers like Japan, Britain, Germany, France, Italy, and Russia. The information I brought back from school was confirmed by my father, who was a teacher of Chinese history. The Opium War in 1840 was a good example of how close China came to being destroyed. The incompetent emperor of the Ching dynasty was forced to sign "hundred-year leases" opening coastal provinces and ports for "free trading." This took place after the foreign soldiers burned down Yuan-ming-yuan — the emperor's magnificent palace in Beijing — and the Allied commander pleased himself with a Chinese prostitute on the empress's bed.

The Japanese invasion in 1937 was another good example of the government's incompetence. It demonstrated what the foreigners were really up to when they talked of "free trading." China was not allowed to say no to their greed. When she did, the "rape" took place. During the Japanese occupation, thirty million Chinese were killed. Just in Nanking alone, the Japanese slaughtered as many as 350,000 people and raped eighty thousand women.

The pictures of heaps of severed heads we were shown as children could not have been more horrifying. In fact there was no need to show them. The memories were recent and fresh. Every family kept its own record of lives lost or damaged. It was Mao who showed China how to stand up to the invaders. It was Mao who saved us from being beheaded, buried alive, bayoneted, raked with machine gun fire, doused with gasoline and burned. No one in China would argue that except my father, who whispered once in a while that the Japanese surrender in 1945 had a lot to do with their defeat in World War II. Besides Mao's effort, the Japanese were pressured to give up China by Stalin's Red Army in Russia. In other words, Mao happened to harvest other people's crops while working on his own. Unfortunately my father's view got him in big trouble. Nevertheless he didn't contradict the fact that Mao was the hero of China. It became natural for people to follow Mao. That was the point of all the education we received at school: to believe in Mao was to believe in China's future. They were the same.

For me it was understandable that Mrs. Pei disagreed with her daughter. Mrs. Pei had been mistreated for marrying a foreigner. But who could easily forget the image of the thousand-year-old imperial palace engulfed in flames? Who could escape the memories of fleeing one's home? Mrs. Pei's experience made her hate Mao. And that was exactly the opposite of where Wild Ginger stood. Wild Ginger couldn't make her mother understand how she felt.

Wild Ginger wanted to be a Maoist, a true Maoist, the one who would save China from disaster. It would be a different kind of Maoist than Hot Pepper's. In my opinion, Hot Pepper took advantage of Maoism and she had no understanding of what being a Maoist meant. Wild Ginger called Hot Pepper a "fake Maoist." I couldn't agree more. Hot Pepper was shouting slogans only to bully her way around, like a fake Buddhist who not only ate meat but also killed. Wild Ginger believed that one day Hot Pepper would be punished for what she had done to ruin Mao's name.

I sat on a little stool by the stove in Wild Ginger's dark kitchen. Wild Ginger was pouring bleach into a water jar.

"What did your father look like?" I asked.

"I'm thinking about burning his picture. You may take a look at it before I light the match."

Wild Ginger put down the bleach and went behind a cupboard. She reached inside a fuse box and searched. Out she came with a tiny mud-colored box. Dusting off the dirt she opened the lid. Inside was a handful of objects: colored soap wrappers, little glass balls, empty matchboxes, Mao buttons, and a palm-size framed photo of a young couple. The woman, although barely recognizable, was Mrs. Pei. Her slanting eyes were bright and filled with a butterfly smile. The man was handsome. A foreigner. He had curly, light-colored hair, a high nose, and deepset eyes.

"Are you shocked?" asked Wild Ginger.

I nodded and admitted that I had never seen a foreigner before.

"You don't think I look like him, do you?"

"Well, you have his nose."

"Why don't you say I have my mother's eyes? I mean they are almond shaped and slanting. They are one hundred percent Oriental."

"Well, that's true. Except the color of your pupils."

"Well, if there were eye dyes, I would dye them black."

"It doesn't bother me the way they are. I like them."

"Anyway, I consider myself lucky."

"Lucky?"

"My eyes are the only things that make me look Chinese. Imagine the other way around!"

"According to Hot Pepper everything that's non-Chinese is reactionary."

"Someday I will roast that bitch."

"Your mother is beautiful."

"She used to be."

"From the photo, she looked happy with your father."

"I suppose she was happy. It's a shame that she has never recovered from his death."

"Your mother is quite ill."

"She is dying. She wants to die. She has stopped going to the hospital. I am not important to her. She talks about disowning me."

"She was just angry at what you said about your father. I am sure she didn't mean it."

"Maple, she shouldn't have given birth to me."

"How could you say that to your mother? You are being unreasonable, Wild Ginger."

Playing with the photo frame she sighed. "The other day the Red Guards came to rob us. They beat Friendly and broke his left leg."

"Is that why he is limping?"

"Yes. Next time when they come Friendly will be hanged, cooked, and eaten."

"No. They won't do that."

"Oh yes. I heard them talking about it."

The thought chilled me. I was silent.

Wild Ginger sat motionless for a while, and then she slowly slid the photo from the frame and lit a match.

"What are you doing? You aren't burning the picture, are you?"

"Stay where you are."

Squatting down, she put the photo over the flame. I drew in my breath but dared not move. The image of her father curled, turned brown, then black. The flame then ate up her mother. The corners of Wild Ginger's mouth tilted into an ironic smile.

The ashes snowed down on the concrete floor.

"Are you afraid, Wild Ginger?" My voice was thin.

"I can't afford to be afraid." She got up and went to the sink. Unpacking a bag of medicinal herbs, she began to wash and prepare them.

"What did your mother do before she met your father?" I asked, trying to distract my fear.

"She worked at the Shanghai People's Opera House. She was their leading singer. She was doing well until my father went to see her play. They fell in love and started their journey to misery."

"Will she perform again?"

"Of course not. She is considered an enemy. She has to

be reformed through hardship. We both have to be re-formed — 'The daughter of a legend gets to be a heroine and the daughter of a rat gets to dig the dirt,' as the saying goes. The interesting thing is that I am guilty and she is not. What I bear is a birth defect. It took me a long time to real-ize that. But Maple, I am not a fatalist. I'm trying to change the course of my life."

I wished that I could tell her that it seemed impossible.

"Watch me, Maple." As if reading my mind she contin-ued. "Someday, I will be a revolutionary. A Maoist star. I will prove that I am just as good and trustworthy as the bravest Maoist. I have made that a promise to myself. No one will stop me from being who I want to be. Not Hot Pepper, not my mother, not the ghost of my father."

Wild Ginger's eyes stared through the kitchen window to the cement wall of her neighbor's house. The wall was painted with a huge smiling Mao head with red rays shoot-ing out from the center. Mao was wearing an army cap with a red star on the top. The sunlight bounced off the paint and onto Wild Ginger, tinting her face red. Her eyes shone brightly. Her hands, which had been washing pots, stopped moving. The tap kept running, the sink was filled. The wa-ter began to spill. She was not aware of it. "No one," she ut-tered.

I felt a deep admiration rise inside me. I reached out my hand and shut off the faucet.

4

It was the end of the class. We were on Mao's "On Protracted War." The noises of other rooms dismissing classes were heard around the campus. Wild Ginger signaled me with her eyes that I should be ready to run. We quietly fastened the straps of our school bags.

The bell rang. I jumped out of the bench and ran to exit the classroom. Wild Ginger followed me. It took her a couple of turns to cut across the seats. She was caught by Titi.

"The reactionaries are slipping away!" Titi screamed.

"Block them!" Hot Pepper ordered. The gang chased. I ran back to assist Wild Ginger. Fists, woodsticks, and blows from an abacus rained down on my head and shoulders.

"Maple!" Wild Ginger pulled me over. Back to back, we punched. We were moving toward the gate successfully.

We were by Chia Chia Lane now. Hot Pepper and the gang had lost sight of us. I gasped hard. Wild Ginger was limping.

"What's wrong with your leg?"

"Hot Pepper got me with her abacus. The sow!"

"She almost poked my eye with her pencil. But I got her too. I broke her pencil in half."

"She threatened to send her three brothers, 'the Dragons.' They are vicious."

"I've heard of them. They work at the Number Seven Lumber Factory and it's said they beat five people to death."

"We must find help, Wild Ginger."

"How?"

"Let's go to the Red Flag Middle School."

"Do you know anyone there?"

"I wonder if he remembers me."

"Who?"

"A Mao activist. Last year's champion of the Mao Quotation-Citing Contest. He is a head of the Red Guards at the school. He is my neighbor."

"How did you meet him?"

"It was in the soy milk shop last Sunday. He was in a hurry to visit his father in the hospital, but the line was three blocks long. He came to me although we had never spoken before. He asked if I would let him cut in. I let him in but the people behind me protested. To shut them up I said that he was my brother. And he got his milk . . . I wonder if he would offer us some protection."

"What's his name?"

"Evergreen."

"Evergreen? How dare he! That's the name of the protagonist in Madame Mao's opera!"

"It's true and I had asked him about it. I asked how dare he copy Madame Mao."

"And what was the reaction?"

"He said she copied *him*. He was given the name at his birth in 1954 and Madame Mao's opera was not conceived until 1960."

"Sounds like he's got character."

"Isn't that interesting!"

We found him. He was writing a big-character poster entitled "What We Talk About When We Talk About Loyalty." He was sixteen years old. Tall with a thin face and a pair of staring single-lid eyes. I didn't know how to describe him when Wild Ginger asked me except that he was handsome. I fell short of words as I considered him. I could say that he gave the impression of possessing an honest character. He was frank — knew exactly what he wanted and asked for it. The neighbors said that he was "square," which meant that he'd been brought up by strict parents. But there was something else about him that struck me. Something mysterious and unusual. He was warm and aloof at the same time. His ability to focus and shift focus without warning intrigued me. He projected a sense that he was eager to engage, yet the boundary he set was Great Wall thick. Physically, he had an athlete's frame. He was lean and his muscles were very pure in outline. He wore a blue Mao jacket and was working, bending over a Ping-Pong table. His calligraphy was masterly and in the Song dynasty style. We watched him and waited until he finished the last stroke. He noticed Wild Ginger, put down his brush pen, and smiled at her. To me the smile was strange and almost affectionate.

Wild Ginger scratched her arm.

Evergreen picked up his brush pen and turned back to his poster. He dipped the pen into a water jar, then looked at Wild Ginger again.

"Am I bothering you?" Wild Ginger scratched her arm again.

"In a way," he smiled.

"What's wrong with me watching you writing a poster? Isn't this supposed to be a public event?"

"Why are you nervous?"

"Why do you keep looking at me?"

"Do I?"

"Do I look like a reactionary?"

"'A straight tree fears no crooked shadows.'" He threw away his pen and straightened up his back. "Forgive me. I'm Evergreen."

"Hello."

"So, are you here to view the big-character posters?"

"Well, not exactly. I'm here with Maple" — Wild Ginger pushed me toward him — "who thought you knew each other."

"Maple! Hello! Sorry I didn't recognize you. You look different."

"It's my Mao jacket. The dye is bad. Every time I wash it the color changes."

"It was blue last time."

"And now it's purple."

"Next time it'll turn brown."

"You can count on that . . . How is your father?"

"He is out of the hospital."

"What did he have?"

"Tuberculosis. He worked as a miner for twenty-eight years."

"Is he getting well?"

"The doctor told him to eat whatever he likes."

"What does that mean?"

"He is not expected to live long."

"I'm sorry to hear that. If there is anything I can do to help, please . . . I can always fetch you the bean milk, for example." Wild Ginger and Evergreen were staring at each other. "Oh, let me introduce you two. This is Wild Ginger, my classmate, my best friend. Evergreen, my neighbor."

"Wild Ginger? That's an unusual name."

"Not as unusual as Evergreen, the Communist party secretary in Madame Mao's famous opera."

"Are you an opera fan?"

Wild Ginger didn't seem to want to answer the question.

"Her mother is," I answered for her. "Her mother is an opera singer."

"My mother is an enemy," Wild Ginger said bluntly.

I turned to her. "What are you doing?"

"Telling facts. So Evergreen doesn't confuse me with who I really am."

"But isn't this a terrible way to introduce oneself?"

"I thought we came to ask for help. Should we tell the truth?" Wild Ginger shot back.

"No, we don't need help." For a strange reason I suddenly changed my mind. I wasn't sure what it was. Something stirred me and my pride rose. It forbade me to be pitied.

"What kind of help, Maple?" Evergreen asked.

"Nothing. Actually, I'm just showing Wild Ginger around. What's new with you, Evergreen?"

Wild Ginger was puzzled. But she followed me.

Pulling the poster to the side Evergreen answered, "I have been preparing for the coming Mao Quotation-Citing Contest. I am trying to recite three hundred pages. I want to upset my own record."

"Ambitious!"

"I suppose that's what devotion and loyalty are all about."

"Can anyone participate?" Wild Ginger asked.

"It's an open contest."

5

"Wild Ginger has been calling you outside the window," Mother said. It was Sunday morning. I was chopping wood and my mother was cooking. "She sounds troubled. Where are you going? Maple, take the garbage with you."

I shot downstairs. Wild Ginger came to me with a tear-stained face. "My mother . . ." she choked.

It was an ongoing rally. Mrs. Pei was the subject of the denunciation. A board hung on her chest reading FRENCH SPY. A middle-aged man wearing dark-framed glasses was reading a criticism aloud. He was clotheshanger thin. His features were donkeylike. His mouth was a child's drawing of a boat sailing above his chin. He shouted, "Down with the French spy and long live Chairman Mao!"

"It'll be over soon." Standing behind the crowd I comforted Wild Ginger.

"Friendly is being cooked in a wok," she said to me without turning her head.

"Now?" I was shocked.

"They took him this morning . . ."

I held out my arms to embrace her.

"Don't touch me!" She pushed me away. "People will see."

"It looks like your mother is fainting," I observed.

"That's what that man wanted. He wants to see her suffer."

"Who is he?"

"Mr. Choo. My mother's ex-admirer. He is an accountant at the fish market. He lost her to my father sixteen years ago."

"How do you know?"

"I read his love letters to Mother. I read all my mother's letters, including my father's. Of course I couldn't understand them. They were in French."

"Where are the letters?"

"Gone."

"You've burned them?"

"They were disgusting."

"Does your mother know?"

Shaking her head, Wild Ginger sat down on the ground. On the makeshift stage Mrs. Pei looked as if she had passed out. She leaned over a chair. Her body was motionless. The organizer pronounced that she was "faking death," and ordered the rally to continue.

Mr. Choo picked up his speech.

The crowd watched.

Wild Ginger closed her eyes and buried her face in her palms.

The sun was getting hotter. My head was steaming.

"Let's go," I said to Wild Ginger.

"I wish she were dead. I wish I were dead," Wild Ginger murmured.

As a form of punishment, Mrs. Pei was ordered to sweep the lanes in the neighborhood. For the first few weeks Mrs. Pei dragged her sick body about and did the work. She got up at four o'clock in the morning and swept until the sun rose. When she was too sick to get out of bed, Wild Ginger took over.

I didn't know that until early one morning when a cat's wail woke me and I opened the window and heard a *sha-sha-sha-sha* sweeping sound. It was still dark. The streetlights colored the tree trunks orange. The whistle of a steam engine came from a distance. The wind tore the old posters off the wall. Papers scratched the cement ground. The sound carried for a great distance, like nobody's shoes walking by themselves. Suddenly I saw a familiar figure moving with a broom.

I don't remember how long I stood by the window. My body hung halfway over the sill. The day was slowly dawning. I heard the steps of the soldiers of the Shanghai Garrison Group jogging. Their barracks were about a mile down the street. The sound was crisp, like hard brushes scrubbing woks.

I didn't realize that Mother had been standing behind me until she softly asked me what got me up so early.

"Wild Ginger is sweeping the lane for her mother."

Mother came behind me and looked. She sighed deeply.

I closed the window and went to put on my clothes and shoes.

"Where are you going?" Mother asked.

"Mama, may I take the broom with me?"

"It is the work for . . . enemies," Mother warned. "Don't get yourself in trouble."

She was wearing a cloth surgical mask and her mother's indigo canvas jacket with worn corners. She had two sleeve cases on each arm and was in her own army boots. I approached her quietly. She collected the garbage, swept it into a bag, and then carried it to a bin. Lifting the lid, she deposited the trash. She then laid her broom on the ground and went to an old well and looked in.

"Wild Ginger," I called.

She turned around. Her eyes asked, What are you doing here? When she saw that I was holding a broom she understood. She took her mask off. "This is none of your business, Maple."

"You won't be able to cover the lanes all by yourself before school."

"Go home, please."

"What are you doing sticking your head in the well?"

"I'm trying to fetch a dead cat."

"Dead what?"

"Cat, a cat."

"It drowned?"

"It's some activist's trick to give my mother a hard time. They want to be able to say that she loafed on the job, on the cleaning, so they can torture her more."

"What if you just leave it there?"

"It will rot and smell."

"It's not your fault."

"Like I said, my mother is in no position to defend herself."

With two brooms working like a pair of giant chopsticks, we got the dead cat out of the well. After we deposited it in the garbage bin Wild Ginger went on to finish sweeping the rest of the lane. I went to the other end. I swept quickly. All my joints participated in a race against the breaking daylight. Soon my arms were sore and blisters were forming on my palms. My shoes were wet from dew. Finally, Wild Ginger and I met in the middle. It was six-thirty. The sun was up.

"See you at school," I said.

She nodded and turned her face away.

Each dawn I came out. We met in the darkest moment of the day. Wild Ginger no longer rejected my help. In school we stuck together like one person and her shadow. In Hot

Pepper's eyes, we had become a two-member gang. She had stopped attacking me and Wild Ginger. It was hard to believe that Hot Pepper didn't call her wolfy brothers. I guessed that, after all, her brothers couldn't come to the school to fight every day. Hot Pepper had learned that Wild Ginger was a desperado who would risk her life to win a moment.

6

The news of the Americans' invasion of Vietnam was on everyone's lips. Taking it as a threat to China, Mao called for "an entire nation in arms; every citizen a soldier!" Within a week our school was turned into a war camp. Every class became a military training program with soldiers from the People's Liberation Army as instructors. We learned wrestling and bayonet stabbing. To build up our strength, the school set out on a month-long hiking trip called "the New Long March." It was an eight-hour-a-day, weight-carrying trip around Shanghai's suburbs. We would pass places like Xinzhuang, Pingzhuang, Lihu, Minghang, then take the ferry across the Huangpu River and travel into the Fengxian agricultural area.

Our bags were thirty-pound bundles stuffed with blankets and necessities for the month. By the time we reached Xinzhuang, many of us had blisters on our feet and shoulders, and severe back and neck aches. The army instructor taught us how to fix our blisters. At every break, I sat down and took out my needles. Raising my foot, I poked through the blisters with a needle. After that I pulled out one of my hairs and routed it through the broken blister, then made a knot on each blister to keep the fluid draining until it dried up by itself. Soon my feet were full of mosquito-like hair knots.

After the city scene faded, the countryside took over, but we were too exhausted to appreciate the landscape. We walked through the rice paddies, farmhouses, and animal barns longing desperately for the next break.

The bundles on our shoulders were getting heavier. Hot Pepper tried to strike up a song to lift our spirits, but no one responded except Wild Ginger.

Wild Ginger was walking behind me. It was the first time we were allowed to participate in a group activity. We were benefiting from Mao's new teaching, "To expand our force, we must unite with people of gray backgrounds, which include the children of the denounced." Wild Ginger was excited. She was singing loudly, "The sky is big but not as big as the power of the Communist party . . ."

By evening a break was ordered. The school stopped in a village called Yichun. The peasants were ordered by their local party boss to provide us with rooms to spend the night. Our class got a coffin room. The empty coffin was for the family's great-grandfather. It was considered a blessing for a man to see his coffin made before he died. Hot Pepper was afraid of the coffin. She took the spot at the farthest end of the room away from the coffin. Wild Ginger laid her stuff right by the coffin, and I took the space next to her. As we finished unpacking we heard a whistle. We were ordered to fetch yecai — leaflike grass — for dinner. Yecai was what the Red Army ate during Mao's Long March in 1934. The point was for us to taste the bitterness in order to deepen our admiration for Mao.

Wild Ginger and I were assigned as a group to look for yecai. We set out toward the west end of a cornfield. Halfway across the field we were struck by a strange fragrance. As we followed the smell, we entered a leafy enclosure where yecai was growing everywhere. It was a thick-leaved plant with tiny yellow flowers on its top. The sun was setting. There was no one around. We started picking. Quickly we filled up our bags.

The farmhouses with straw tops were dyed orange by the golden sunbeams. The large oil-bearing plants bent down heavily. The smell of yecai thickened. Wild Ginger and I decided to take a break. We put our bags to the side and sat down to enjoy the fragrance. Within a few minutes the sky turned dark and the stars began to glow.

"Look at the moon." Wild Ginger pointed at the sky. "Like a guilty face it keeps burying itself behind the drifting clouds."

"A face? Whose face?"

"My father's," she giggled.

"I don't think the face looks guilty," I said. "It looks rather sad to me."

"Sad? Well, if only the moon could argue."

"The air is sweet."

"It's so quiet here."

"Don't you feel like breaking the silence?"

"Wanna sing?"

"I don't have a good voice."

"Who cares!"

"I do. I would like to have a nice voice like Wild Ginger."

"You know what my mother said? 'That French-head had a good voice.'"

"You mean your father?"

"My mother told me that he liked to put out the lights and sing in the dark."

"Did you ever hear your father sing?"

"I don't remember. My mother says I did. My mother sang me his songs. She wants me to remember him. But who wants to remember a reactionary?"

"What about your voice?"

"I sing all right . . . Well, I love to sing, in fact."

"Would you sing me something?"

"Of course not."

"You have shown me how your father looked, now if you sing I might get an idea of how he sounded."

"I have to go, Maple. I have to go to the restroom badly. But there is no such place."

"Just squat down. Do what the peasants do."

Wild Ginger wandered around for a while and disappeared from my sight.

I lay down on my back. The night was broad and wide. I

began to think about my father. I missed him terribly. As my mind wandered the sweetness of the air disappeared. I became uncomfortable. I felt the sky turn into a broad palm and press itself upon my face. A nameless anxiety crept up on me. I worried about my future. I thought about the word "escape." I wanted to escape school and my family. I wanted to be a Maoist. I understood that it was the only path to a good future. One had to be a Maoist to get a good job. But on the other hand I was confused. I was not sure whether being a Maoist would make me happy. I was not looking forward to graduation. I didn't see a future as bright as the one Chairman Mao promised. Maybe it was the daily hunger, the hardship, that stressed me. And my father. The way he was treated. My family was never enthusiastic about participating in the Cultural Revolution. All my siblings were considered politically nearsighted. I didn't see where it was all leading. Anyhow, Evergreen's record as the Mao-citing champion impressed Wild Ginger more than it did me.

I heard singing. For a brief moment I was sure that I was imagining it. The voice was silky, pure and penetrating. It was in a foreign language. The strangeness grabbed me. Wild Ginger. What was she singing? French? She sang it as if she knew the language. But she didn't. I knew she didn't.

The singing went on for a while and then stopped. Wild Ginger reappeared.

"Was it weird?"

"I liked it. A lot."

"It's a spy code," she teased.

"Then why do you sing it?"

"Just to show you what my mother rubbed my ears with, though she has stopped since the revolution."

"What are the songs about?"

"I have no idea."

"You're lying. Your mother must have explained them to you."

"All right, she did. She said they were about love. The lyrics are disgusting and poisonous."

"I think they are beautiful."

"Don't be stupid, Maple."

"It's true. It shows how much you miss your father."

"You don't know French."

"You don't either."

"What makes you think that I miss him?"

"Your voice."

She paused, as if surprised.

"I really like your voice," I continued.

"You'd like it better if I sang 'I Am Missing Chairman Mao.' I can sound as good as the radio."

Before I could tell her that I had been bored with that song and its constant repetition on the radio and at ceremonies, she turned toward the field to sing with her full voice:

> I raise my head to see the Big Dipper.
> I am missing you, Chairman Mao.
> Longing for you I strive,

Thinking about you I find light in darkness,
Thinking about you I gain my strength.
I owe you my life,
I owe you my happiness.

Deep in the fields moonbeams sparkled overhead. The white rays silently spread, in rushing streams, bathing the corn.

We had yecai as dinner. It was boiled in a wok and mixed with wild sandy-brown rice. The color was exactly manurelike. Many of us threw up before forcing it down our throats. One hour after eating the chamber-pot room was crowded.

"Wild Ginger, I think I like the French song better," I whispered to her after we got into bed and the light was off. "Especially now that you've told me that it was a song your father sang."

"Maple, please, don't bring up that French ghost."

"Well, it helps me to fight the urge to throw up."

"From now on you can mention anything else but the ghost."

"The ghost is in your own voice, Wild Ginger. But I prefer to see it as a fairy."

She turned over and threw a fistful of wheat she had brought back from the field in my face. It shut me up. After a while she said, "Actually, for your information, my ability to memorize is a true gift. My eyes easily store everything they see."

"Well, then you should explore your talent."

"I am working on it. Wanna know a secret? I've been planning to take the championship from Evergreen."

"You mean the Mao Quotation-Citing Contest?"

"Do I surprise you?"

"You talk big."

"Just watch me."

"Silence!" Hot Pepper's voice. "Let's say good night to Chairman Mao and wish him a long, long life."

"Page four hundred and eleven, paragraph one, 'The American imperialism is a paper tiger . . .'" Wild Ginger woke me up at midnight reciting Mao loudly in her dreams.

7

The noise of cicadas pierced the noon heat. I sat in the classroom and worried about Wild Ginger. She was absent. I decided to pay her a visit after school. I thought she probably was caught up in the preparation for the Mao Quotation-Citing Contest.

I passed Chia Chia Lane and saw that Wild Ginger's door was wide open. To my surprise, I saw that Mrs. Pei's plants were crushed and lay scattered around the yard. Strangers were coming in and out of the house. A group of men carried things out — woks, pillows, kitchenware, and toilet paper. They loaded the goods in tricycles and then rode away. I drew near. I didn't recognize these people. They had Red Guard armbands and spoke Mandarin with a northern accent. "Get out of the way!" One of them yelled at me. I moved to the side and saw my neighbor One-Eye Grandpa, a retired veteran, standing by the corner watching. He was eighty-one years old. His left eye had been poked out by a Japanese bayonet during the war. He usually did nothing but walk around the neighborhood all day.

"What's going on, Grandpa?" I went up to him.

"Don't get involved, child."

"I'm Wild Ginger's friend."

"Oh, Wild Ginger. Poor girl. *Zuonieya!* Buddha above, may your eyes open."

"I need to know what's going on, Grandpa. I beg you to tell me. A long life to you. May Chairman Mao grant you good luck."

"Does it matter? I'm tired of living, tired of seeing anyway," he murmured. "There was a letter from France addressed to Mrs. Pei but it got caught by the post office. They turned it over to the authorities. Next thing Mrs. Pei got arrested. She was escorted to the detention house."

"What's the letter about?"

"Who knows! I'm sure Mrs. Pei didn't even get to read it. I would guess it's from the grandparents. It's only natural that they wonder about their granddaughter."

"Where is Wild Ginger?"

"I haven't seen her. She's probably hiding somewhere. She fought with these strangers until she was pushed out."

"Who are these people?"

"Hooligans in Mao jackets!"

"Where are they from?"

"I have no idea. What I can tell you is that it's the fourth bunch. The first bunch was sent by the local authority. They took the books, letters, and photo albums. The second bunch came from the opera house. They took clothes and furniture. The third bunch was from the outer province. They took food, coal, and blankets. Now it's everybody's land."

It wasn't until evening that I saw a big, snakelike creature sitting in the crook of the fig tree. It was my friend. "Wild Ginger!" I cried out.

She didn't answer me. Her head was hidden in leaves.

"Wild Ginger, what are you doing up there?"

"Waiting for my mother."

"Have you . . . have you eaten?"

"I am not hungry."

"Get down. Come with me to my house."

"Leave me alone."

"Come on. You don't want me to come up and get you, do you? You know I am a poor climber."

Finally she began to climb down but she had no strength.

"Wild Ginger!"

"I'll be fine, Maple," she uttered.

I stretched out my arms to help her.

"I am dizzy, Maple. My head . . . Damn." Before she finished her sentence her body slid down like a soft noodle. She passed out in my arms. I held her with all my might and pushed her up against the tree trunk. Turning around I squatted down. I let her fall on my back. Slowly, I stood up and started walking toward my house.

"Buddha above, may your eyes open!" One-Eye Grandpa sighed loudly behind me.

Wild Ginger woke. She was lying on the floor — our family bed. My mother offered her a cup of water while my sisters wiped her limbs with hot towels.

Wild Ginger tried to sit up, but Mother stopped her. "You're too weak. Go back to sleep if you can."

"I can't."

"Well, child, you have to. Your mother would demand it. I am treating you as I would Maple."

Wild Ginger lay back down.

"Maple" — Mother passed me a letter as she went to wipe the table — "your father's. Said he's not allowed to return until New Year's."

I was greatly disappointed. But it was not the first time I'd experienced such disappointment. I tried to remember what my father taught me, to think positively. "So Wild Ginger can stay here then. She can sleep in Father's spot."

Mother pulled me aside and whispered, "We've run out of food. I have sold everything. I was hoping your father . . ."

"Mama, we can just keep eating one meal a day and drinking water when we're hungry. I'll go to the market to search through the garbage bins. I always get lucky on Tuesdays. They have new workers then who prepare the vegetables carelessly. There are a lot of half-rotten leaves thrown away. They are perfectly edible!"

"I am not sure. Your little brother has a bladder infection. The hospital bill took all my salary this month and the money I had borrowed from your aunt. Your grandmother refuses to come to visit because she sees that we can't afford an extra mouth."

"How many yuan do we have left?"

"Six."

"We've got seven days left in the month. Six divided by . . . it's eighty-five cents per day. I will try to manage it. Twenty-four cents for the noodles, twenty cents for rice, fourteen cents for squashes, three cents for vegetables, three cents for beans . . ."

"Are you feeding ants?" Mother shook her head.

I kept going. "One cent for scallions. And Mama, we have about twenty cents left for meat!"

"Twenty cents for meat!" Mother laughed bitterly. "That will be paper thin."

The light outside the windows had disappeared. Mother hurried us to go to sleep. We all lay down next to one another. Wild Ginger was sandwiched between me and my younger sister.

It was close to midnight when Wild Ginger woke me up. "Are you citing the quotations again?" I asked. She didn't answer but continued, "'. . . To attack the reactionary we must be merciless, we must not think of them as humans but wolves, snakes, and locusts. It is either us or them . . .'" Her eyes were tightly closed.

I gently pinched her nose. She stopped reciting. I tried to

go back to sleep. The moonlight bathed the room in blue. Everything was visible. My brother's Mao statue stood on top of the closet. The Mao portrait stared down from the wall. We had Mao stuff in every corner of the house. Portraits, nine of them. Mao's image was printed on book covers, closets, blankets, windows, towels, plates, cups, containers, and bowls. I was getting sick of staring and being stared at by Mao all the time. But I dared not complain. Mother had taught me the ancient wisdom — "Disaster comes with your tongue." It was especially true today. Any neighbor could be a watchdog for the government. If we had no Mao portraits on the wall we would have been considered anti-Maoists. I remembered Mother once hung a colorful picture of children playing in a lotus pond on the wall. It had green leaves and pink flowers. I asked her where the picture was and she wouldn't give me a straight answer.

My eyes landed on the floor where my father's letter lay. Mother had been reading the letter over and over. I began to imagine what my father was doing at this moment. He would be missing us. He was serving his punishment for being outspoken. He was a teacher in Chinese history. The party secretary in his work unit reported to his superiors that he had views which contradicted Mao's teaching. The next thing we knew he was named a "dangerous thinker." Since he'd been sent to the labor collective, his sixty-nine-yuan salary had been cut down to fifteen yuan. He sent thirteen yuan home every month.

What would he be eating? Yecai? I imagined my father

thinner now. He was a good father and had a great sense of humor. In his letter he called himself "a phoenix who got his feathers pulled, thus uglier than a hen, but still a phoenix." My mother had the opposite character. She was a worrier. She called herself "a headless fly."

In her sleep Wild Ginger's hands clenched my arm. I tried to relax her fingers. But she pulled me more tightly. It was as if she were drowning. Her grip was desperate. What would she be dreaming? Champion of the Mao Quotation-Citing Contest?

Pushing herself to be a Maoist had become Wild Ginger's obsession. Was she as strong as she thought? I didn't believe that she really hated her father. If she did, his image wouldn't be kept so vividly in her mind. In her thoughts, not only did he breathe, he sang. She had to denounce him every day in order to push him away from her. If she hated him, she would have stopped talking about him. She wouldn't act so hurt when her mother mentioned his name; it was as if salt were being poured on a fresh wound. She wouldn't have memorized his songs, in French, in his native tongue. They came to her so naturally. Maybe the truth was quite different. Maybe the truth was that she loved her father, so much that she was punishing herself for loving him.

Would she be dreaming about him now? What would she see him doing? Bringing antiques home? She once told me that he was an antique collector. She remembered that he brought home a wooden ball with ninety-nine dragons carved on its surface, which she broke accidentally. He was about to spank her but dropped his hand when she threw herself at him and held his knee. She remembered parting from him in the hospital. No one informed her that he was dying. He was speaking French to her mother and she remembered that her mother kept nodding, unable to utter a sound. She tried to figure out what they were saying, but it was impossible. Finally her father turned to her. He was smiling, but she saw his tears glistening. He didn't say goodbye. He was unable to. Her mother didn't bring her to the funeral. Her father just disappeared. Suddenly and forever. She remembered that she joked when told that he was dead. "What about the antiques? Did he expect me to take care of those?" Later on when she was told that he was a spy she almost wanted to believe it, for she thought he had deserted her.

The air was cooling but it felt sticky. The blanket we all shared got pulled to one side. It looked like it was floating on top of a sea. The moon's reflection paved a flowing path across the waves. After midnight there was wind. Moonlight came through the window and spread itself on Wild Ginger's face like a veil.

8

From One-Eye Grandpa, Wild Ginger learned that the looters were gone. She went back to her house to check on her mother. We promised to meet at the school, but after the bells rang she still hadn't shown up. I kept my eyes on the door. Finally she appeared. She looked ill. Her hair was messy. Dragging her bag and abacus, she walked toward her seat. Sitting down she took out her books and pencil box absent-mindedly. The class had been following Mrs. Cheng's calculations on a giant abacus hung from the board. I was eager to make eye contact with Wild Ginger, but she avoided me. She focused her attention on Mrs. Cheng's abacus and practiced the numbers on her own. The sound of fingers tabbing abacuses was loud in the room. Mrs. Cheng stopped before the conclusion of the day. She asked if anyone would like to give the answer. Wild Ginger raised her hand. She was called. She gave a correct answer but her voice was a little odd, choked.

"Are you all right, Wild Ginger?" Mrs. Cheng asked.

Wild Ginger nodded. She quickly sat back down and buried her head in her notebook. It didn't escape me that she was trying to hold back tears.

When the class was dismissed, Wild Ginger threw her school bag over her shoulder and ran toward the gate. "Wild Ginger!" I chased her. She shot out like an arrow. To get away from me she slashed through the bushes. I sensed that something terrible had happened.

I followed her. Finally she tripped over a cracked curb and fell. I caught up with her and motioned her toward me. She turned away and yelled angrily, "Go away, Maple!"

"Don't make me an enemy." I pulled her to a quiet lane on the side road behind a garbage dump. "We are each other's last ally."

"Leave me alone!"

"Not until I find out what's going on."

She pushed me. Seeing that I was determined to stay, she took out her pencil box. Her body was shaking violently and she was gasping. "If you don't leave me alone . . ." She opened the pencil box lid and picked out a pencil. She then squatted down with her back against the wall. Suddenly she placed her left hand on her knee and stabbed.

The pencil tip broke inside the back of her hand.

"Wild Ginger!"

As if feeling nothing she repeated her action.

I was stunned.

She put the broken pencil back in the box and picked up a pencil knife.

"Don't! I am leaving! Put down the knife!" I backed myself step by step toward the entrance of the lane. My mind was blank. I saw traces of blood dripping from Wild Ginger's hand, down to her pants and then her shoes. My frustration overwhelmed me. Suddenly I was scared.

She looked in my direction. But she didn't see me. Her eyes were telling me that she was in another world, or was going there. She looked unafraid. I remembered what my mother had told me about how one became insane: "One thought got knotted in the ball of nerves."

"Keep walking, Maple!" Wild Ginger shouted.

I marched on. My legs didn't feel like mine. As I passed the gate of the lane, a sudden convulsion squeezed my guts. It was like a blunt cleaver cutting through my skin. I stopped and turned around. I ran back toward Wild Ginger. All my thoughts came back and rushed into one point where reason no longer existed. "Stab me, Wild Ginger! Stab me! You devil!" I threw myself at her.

Bursting with fury, Wild Ginger raised her abacus and smashed it against the garbage dump. When the beads rolled all over, she came and grabbed me by the collar. She stared, her eyebrows twisted into a knot.

What was I seeing? They were a blind man's eyes. Big and wide but without focus.

I was numb at first, then slowly I felt that I was breaking like a ceramic wok on a hot stove — the liquid seeped through the cracks to sizzle in the tongues of flame.

"You are the only friend I've got," my voice pleaded involuntarily. "I can't take Hot Pepper's umbrella anymore.

Wild Ginger, I am not as strong as you are. I need you. I can't have you go mad. You must not go mad . . ."

The hand on my collar loosened. The blind man's eyes came back into focus. Tears welled up and gushed down her pale cheeks.

"Maple, my mother . . . hanged herself."

9

Wild Ginger tried to appear calm after her mother died, but the sorrow weighed her spirit down. She came to school every day wearing a black armband and a white paper flower in her hair. She showed little grief in public. She competed with Hot Pepper on Mao quotation reciting and laughed when she scored high. I observed her quietly. I found her smile forced. I tried to stay as close to her as possible.

Although Wild Ginger no longer had to sweep the lane for her mother, she faced serious financial trouble. The neighborhood committee allowed her to continue to live in her house but would provide no aid for her expenses. She had to come up with money for utility bills and she had no relatives — all of them had separated themselves from her to avoid suspicion in order to protect their own families. Learning the situation, Mrs. Cheng talked to the authorities. She mentioned Wild Ginger's score on Mao study, which was the highest in the district. The principal agreed to reduce Wild Ginger's tuition from twelve yuan to eight yuan. Still Wild Ginger had to come up with the rest of the money.

My mother offered Wild Ginger food in our house. "There won't be much, but you can eat what we eat."

Wild Ginger declined the offer. "I have found something to do to earn money," she said to me. "I found a job as a seafood preparer. I have already spoken to the neighborhood committee and obtained a permit to set up a stall at the market from three to seven in the morning. When people buy seafood I will prepare it for them in exchange for unwanted fish skin, heads, tails, and intestines. I will sell the beltfish scales to the chemical refinery for two cents a pound; I will sell the fish heads, tails, and intestines to families with cats for one cent a pile, I will sell the squid spines to herb shops for two cents a pound. And I will cut the butts of snails for three cents a pound."

Although her voice was filled with enthusiasm, my tears welled up. I knew exactly what kind of hardship she would have to endure to carry out her plans. Before everything else, she had to get up at two o'clock each morning to secure herself a working spot. She had to fight for her business among other seafood preparers. The winter had come. It had been fifteen below zero. When I got up to go to the market at five I got frostbite all over my hands and feet. I was outside for only a half-hour, and I was walking and moving. Imagine squatting on the icy ground for hours on end, fingers in cold water and pulling frozen fish intestines. For all her struggle she would earn only a few cents a day.

"I am glad that you have figured it all out," I murmured.

"Don't worry," she said with appreciation.

"The market won't officially open till five-thirty, which means that you'll have to wait in the cold to guard your spot for three and a half hours."

"I'll make use of the time," she said. "I'll practice reciting Mao quotations."

I was unable to hold in my sadness. I went to Evergreen to tell him about Wild Ginger. He was silent after I finished speaking. He said that our best help would be to check on her every now and then. "Tell her that if she needs me to help her in preparing for the Mao Quotation-Citing Contest I will feel privileged."

The month of December went by quickly. My father was allowed to join the family for the New Year. Mother wanted us to spend as much time with him as possible. She took up all the housework, including going to the market. My father sent us children out to the recycling station to collect books on history. Most of those books were looted goods. The Red Guards had removed them from the shelves of houses and libraries. They burned most of the books and dumped the rest in the trash. The pickers fetched them from bins and sold them to the station by the pound. My father wanted to buy some of the books back. He thought that it was a good deal to buy books by the pound. At five cents per pound, he could get an average of four books for under ten cents. "What do you say when the comrade in charge asks why you'd like to buy the books?" my father drilled us.

"To use as toilet paper!" we answered in one voice.

I was kept busy. Not a day passed that I didn't think about Wild Ginger. Especially during New Year's Eve dinner when all family members and relatives gathered at the table and the firecrackers started to brighten the sky. The school was closed for the holidays and I hadn't seen Wild Ginger for weeks. I wondered how she had been doing with her stall. The last time we parted at the school, I invited her to come over to celebrate New Year's Eve. She accepted, but her tone was reluctant. When I asked why, she confessed that she wouldn't want to be reminded that she was all alone. "Well, do what you feel like then," I responded. "My door will always be open to you."

She didn't come for dinner. And I missed her. I asked mother if tomorrow I could go and buy father's favorite food — snails. "I'll have them prepared in the market."

"It takes too long to have the snails' butts removed. One pound takes about one hour. Unless you don't mind waiting," Mother said.

"I sure don't," I said happily and went to sleep early that night.

It was three o'clock in the morning when I woke. The night was icy. The wind that came through the windowsills sounded like an old woman sobbing. I took my clothes and got off the bed. My legs were trembling in the cold. I picked up my socks from the floor. They were like two frozen fish. I stood on them and crunched the ice before I put them on. My toes ached with the numbing cold. I pushed my feet into my shoes. Taking a basket I stepped out of the door. The streets were wrapped in darkness. I walked fast toward the market. The wind on my skin felt like tiny cutting knives. Soon I saw the light from the market's bare bulbs. I went to check the fish booth first. There were already lines of people encircling the booth. A man with a stub of chalk wrote numbers on people's sleeves to make sure no late-comers would cut in. I got my number and put down my basket. My fingers were beginning to freeze. Like everyone else I stamped my feet and wiggled my toes to keep warm.

The clerk at the fish booth took out a big wooden hammer. He chopped an ice pack of fish and eels. The stinking smell indicated that the seafood was not fresh. Most of the fish were already rotten. The squid had big bones and paper-thin flesh. The beltfish, too, were stick thin. Only the snails looked all right.

The wind rose. It almost blew my basket away. I picked up a couple of rocks from the side street and placed them inside the basket to hold it. I asked the woman behind me to watch my spot. I said that I needed to pee and would be right back.

I found Wild Ginger's stall in the middle of a group of seafood preparers. They were on the side of the market where the wind blew like slashing whips. Wild Ginger was bundled in scarves and rags. Sitting on a small stool, she held a Mao Quotation Book in her hands. She was wearing a pair of fingerless gloves. Two pieces of plastic, tied at her knees, shielded her lower legs. In front of her a washboard lay flat side up. On top of it rested a pair of rusty scissors and a crook-toothed knife. Three metal buckets stood in front of her. I assumed that one would be for fish scales, another for squid bones, and the third for heads, tails, and intestines. Next to the buckets was a jar covered with a piece of towel. I assumed that it was warm water.

The bell rang. I rushed back to my spot and picked up my basket. The crowd began to push forward. The fish booth was sealed by the human wall. The line moved slowly. Everyone watched the pile of fish getting smaller and smaller. We all prayed that there would be some left for us. "It looks like you will be the last," the woman behind me said. "Would you let me have a little for watching your spot for you? My daughter-in-law just had a baby."

I nodded. My turn came. The squid were gone. The eels were gone too. There was only one beltfish left. I passed the fish to the woman and ordered the rest of the snails. It was about a pound and a half. The human wall around me collapsed in disappointed sighs. The clerk began to scrub and wash the booth.

My feet landed in front of Wild Ginger. She was busy preparing a beltfish. Using the knife she skillfully scrubbed off the silver-colored scales and deposited them in the bucket. Then she picked up the scissors and started to take out the intestines. Once in a while she dipped her fingers in the warm water. I was sure the water was icy cold by now. There were a few cuts on her fingers. They were bleeding.

"Are my snails ready yet?" a customer asked Wild Ginger.

"Coming up," Wild Ginger answered apologetically without raising her head. "I've already cut half and I'll finish the rest in a minute after this one."

"My snails were here before someone else's fish," the customer complained. "I thought you said first come first served. You are a liar and I won't come to you again."

"I'm terribly sorry, madam," Wild Ginger said as she put the fish in one basket and picked up the snails. She talked with her hands moving fast. The snails dropped into the basket as if from a machine.

I moved up. My basket was right by her head. "Service, madam?" She pulled over my basket. "I am good and quick. I charge a cent cheaper." She was talking to me.

"I'll never come to you again," the snail lady complained. "You haven't finished with one customer and you have started to grab another. How greedy!"

Wild Ginger tried to move her fingers faster. The blisters on her palm and around her fingers looked swollen. The blood from her cuts mixed with the eels'. Wild Ginger's scarf got blown off by the wind. She reached out her right leg to hold the scarf down while her fingers continued to work with the snails. "Madam, I'll give you one cent back for the delay."

"You ought to," the woman said.

"Wild Ginger," I called.

She raised her head. "Maple!" She turned to the lady. "She is no customer. She's my friend."

"Hurry up!" The woman was irritated.

"Thanks for the business. Thanks for waiting." Wild Ginger was talking to me.

"May I help?" I offered.

"I'm almost done. Don't dirty your hands. The stink will stick to you all day. Here you are, madam, done." She shoveled the finished snails into the customer's basket.

The woman gave Wild Ginger a dirty look. She threw three cents to her and walked away.

Wild Ginger began to work on my snails as I went to fetch vegetables. By now the day was bright. The market was much less crowded. Most of the booths were empty. The late customers looked miserable — there was nothing except frozen radishes to buy. People had been eating radishes for months.

By the time I came back, Wild Ginger was selling her cat food. She piled the fish heads, tails, and intestines neatly on the washed-clean board and waited for the customers. She sat on a piece of brick and saved her stool for me. A couple of old ladies came and bargained.

I sat down next to Wild Ginger. I was hungry and frozen. I'd love to have a bowl of hot tofu soup, I thought. But I dared not spend the money. I was sure Wild Ginger was hungrier. The smell of baked yams wafted over. Wild

Ginger got up and yelled, "Cat food!" Her eyes sought eagerly. "Fresh intestines!" She rubbed her hands to warm them. Her nose was red. Her cheeks were splotched with black squid ink. Fish scales glinted in her hair. She yawned and stretched her arms and legs.

"The other day, Evergreen came to visit," Wild Ginger told me. "He helped me with the Mao reciting and dropped a lot of tips, even knowing that I was a rival."

"I told you he was a nice fellow."

"He said the purpose of the contest was not to win but to promote Mao study. He was impressed by my work. He thought that I had a good chance to win."

"I agree, Wild Ginger. You work so hard."

"There was something else Evergreen said that disturbed me."

"What is it?"

"It's Hot Pepper. Do you know Hot Pepper has registered for the contest too? She said that she was determined to beat me. But she's no match. So she uses political excuses to make sure I won't enter."

"The spy stuff again?"

"What else can she say?"

"This is going to be tricky."

"I know. Evergreen is fighting for me. He believes that the Communist party promotes justice and fairness. And I believe him."

The tinkling of bells reached our ears. Two bicycles with large containers hung on each side arrived. They were the refinery and herb shop workers. Wild Ginger went up to greet them.

"It's not fresh. I don't want it," the refinery man bargained.

"I haven't gone home yet, big uncle," Wild Ginger negotiated. "You won't get fresher stuff this morning."

"One cent a pound."

"Two cents, uncle. I have to eat too."

"One cent or I am leaving." The man rang his bell.

"Fine, one cent." Wild Ginger gave the man her buckets.

"The squid bone is too small, I don't want it," the herb man said, ringing his bell too, as if hurrying to move on.

"Half price. One cent a pound," Wild Ginger yielded.

The man took out his scale, weighed the bucket, then paid Wild Ginger. "You smart kid. You know I'm your last stop."

Wild Ginger counted the money and placed the pennies carefully inside her pocket. She looked satisfied and went to close her stall.

I said goodbye and walked toward home. I tried to fight against a welling sorrow. My mornings were never the same after that day. I thought of Wild Ginger while I indulged in warm blankets. I thought of her while drinking my mother's hot tofu soup. In learning to appreciate my family's luck I experienced a sense of guilt. I was in tears while my mother put a piece of beltfish in my bowl, and while my father awarded me with a story read from the book I got him from the recycling station. Bathing in my parents' attention, I understood the word "deprivation." I wished Wild Ginger well, I wished that she could continue to rise as the star of the Mao study, and I wished that her fish-smell hands would eventually bring her a good future. I felt that I owed her, that society owed her. She had to win. And I would do anything to help her win.

10

The Mao Quotation-Citing Contest was broadcast live throughout the district, with every class-room tuned in. It was a clear spring day. I sat at my desk and concentrated on listening to the loudspeaker. The scores of the final contestants were close. By the afternoon there were only three left — Hot Pepper, Evergreen, and Wild Ginger. The result wasn't hard to guess since Wild Ginger's lead was great. Suddenly the judge, the district party secretary, ordered a recess and said that the winner would be announced the next morning.

I was very excited for Wild Ginger. The winner of the contest was to go on to a national-level competition. If she won, she could be honored as a Maoist. She might even be brought to meet Chairman Mao himself.

I went to Wild Ginger's house and waited for her return from the People's Square, where the contest took place. It was dark already. I sat by her door. One hour passed. I saw no shadow of her. I paced back and forth along Chia Chia

Lane and hoped to run into her. Finally it was not Wild Ginger but my oldest brother who came.

"Quick, sis, there has been a fight." My brother tried to catch his breath. "Hot Pepper and her brothers have gotten Wild Ginger. Fortunately she was with Evergreen."

My brother led me to the spot. I saw Wild Ginger chasing away Yaya to the end of the lane. Two of Hot Pepper's brothers were lying on the ground. Evergreen had Hot Pepper's oldest brother, Big Dragon, underneath him. Under the streetlight Evergreen's face was distorted. He had a swollen jaw. I assumed that the fighting had been fierce. Big Dragon begged for mercy. Hot Pepper was crying and throwing herself at Evergreen. Evergreen twisted Big Dragon's arms backward.

"You are breaking his arms," Hot Pepper screamed.

Evergreen clenched his teeth. "You've started the biting and now you'd better swallow the whole cake!"

"Wild Ginger had no right to compete in the first place," Hot Pepper yelled. "She is politically disqualified."

"The party gives equal rights to every comrade who devotes himself to Chairman Mao," Evergreen shot back.

"A spy is not a comrade —"

Unexpectedly Hot Pepper's mouth was slapped by her youngest brother, Little Dragon. "Go home, sis."

Evergreen let go of Big Dragon.

Middle Dragon and Little Dragon came to help their brother up, then took off.

"We'll be back!" Hot Pepper shouted.

"If your brothers dare to touch Wild Ginger again I'll pull off their squid heads!"

Wild Ginger looked like a blooming lotus. Evergreen took us to a tofu soup stand for a snack. We wolfed down steamed buns. I couldn't help staring at Wild Ginger. It was the first time I'd seen her happy. We finished the soup quickly and started walking. She took my hand and walked quietly on my right side while Evergreen was on my left. Wild Ginger didn't thank Evergreen. Didn't even look at him. We were silent.

"Who do you think will be the winner?" I broke the silence.

"It ought to be Wild Ginger," said Evergreen. "But I have a feeling the district party secretary is having his doubts."

"It was my fear," Wild Ginger sighed. "How naive I was to believe —"

"You must trust the Communist party," Evergreen interrupted. "You must trust Chairman Mao. Very few people are crooks."

We were at the crossing next to a bicycle parking lot. Evergreen went to pick up his bicycle.

"How do you solve the problem, Evergreen?" I grew impatient.

Without taking his eyes off Wild Ginger, Evergreen said, "You have to learn to endure the test of time. You have to be the winner of hearts and not just the contest. The truth is" — he hesitated for a second and then pressed on — "you've already taken the championship in my heart."

Wild Ginger's cheeks flushed.

As if embarrassed by his own frankness, Evergreen backed off and got on the bicycle. He nodded a goodbye and disappeared into the traffic.

It surprised everyone when the winner was announced the next day. Evergreen won first place, with Hot Pepper second. Wild Ginger got an honorable mention. Mrs. Cheng received an explanation from the authorities, which she read to the class. Wild Ginger lost her place because of her poor background. She was given the school's and the district authorities' regrets. It seemed that everyone understood and accepted the treatment given to Wild Ginger. Since she was a second-class citizen, Wild Ginger's suffering became insignificant. If she were recognized as a dog, it was only natural for her to drink water from a puddle instead of a cup.

Before I had a chance, Evergreen went to comfort Wild Ginger. He went to visit her every couple of days and later on went to help her in the fish market in the mornings. When I asked him about his feelings toward the outcome he spoke almost angrily. Besides his complaint on the unfairness of the contest, he felt betrayed by the district party secretary. As he tried to comfort Wild Ginger, convincing her to rely on the party's judgment, he himself was not convinced. He became disillusioned, even disgusted.

"I feel devastated that Wild Ginger not only accepted the treatment, but also embraced it," Evergreen said to me. "She believes that she just has to try harder to prove herself . . . I somehow see it as being more destructive than constructive. I demanded a conversation with the district party secretary."

"And?" I asked eagerly.

"He said taking risks or being experimental was never his style."

"What does that mean?"

"He couldn't promote a spy's daughter as a revolutionary model."

"Why didn't he make that clear before the contest?"

"He wanted to use Wild Ginger, to earn his own political credit in the party. You see, he took the chance to show how far he could push a young mind to memorize Mao."

"So Wild Ginger was made a fool."

"Yes, shamefully." He paused. After a while he added, "So was I."

"Mao's representatives." I couldn't help being sarcastic.

"My disappointment was so great that I no longer see things the same way, Maple. Inside I feel sick, depressed. It was not just remorse for Wild Ginger's loss. It was something deeper, more dangerous, and I am frightened of its result."

11

In 1971 we turned fifteen. Wild Ginger and I graduated from July First Elementary School and entered the Red Flag Middle School. The curriculum was the same, with Mao study still the priority. Wild Ginger had learned the whole business of the seafood market. She knew the names of every wholesaler, fisherman, retailer, market employee, and employer in the market. She knew their habits, families, and relations. She even got to know her mother's ex-admirer, accountant Mr. Choo. After Mrs. Pei died, Mr. Choo appeared to feel guilty. He brought Wild Ginger food and presents, trying to reconcile. Wild Ginger was unmoved. The man explained that he had to betray his own conscience in order to survive. Wild Ginger spat in his face and walked away.

Wild Ginger took me to hang out at the fish market afternoons and evenings. We helped the employees stocking up the supplies. When asked why we were there, Wild Ginger quoted Mao's teaching, "'The youth should get themselves out of the classrooms and learn directly from the working class.'" She made friends with many of the fishwomen, who transported loads of seafood from the ports to the city on their tricycles. They were simple and delightful although poorly educated. They had large muscles and big feet.

Wild Ginger admired the fishwomen's spirit. She became very friendly with a young one named Jung, who was sixteen. She had a round face and heavyset body. She always brought Wild Ginger pieces of dried fish to chew.

Although I didn't particularly like the fish market — its smell bothered me and made me nauseous — I went for Wild Ginger's sake. After a while I found myself interested in the conversations between Jung and Wild Ginger. I learned a lot by listening to their discussions on the nature of the sea, seaweed, fish, squid, snails, and the techniques to catch them.

The year went by quickly. It didn't occur to me until summer that Jung looked worn down. She'd lost her cheerfulness, was nervous, and didn't seem to trust herself. Wild Ginger didn't tell me anything until I remarked on Jung's appearance.

"She hasn't been careful keeping track of her shipments," Wild Ginger said. "Accountant Choo found out that she often brought in less than she had loaded. It's the fifth time that she was missing two baskets of beltfish."

"Is it possible to lose them on her way?"

"It is. But since she's been paying attention she is sure there must be some mistake. But still, she was short of baskets when she passed Mr. Choo's scale."

"That's odd."

"Something is smelly about Accountant Choo," Wild Ginger said. "I have been watching him. I suspect that he is taking advantage of Jung. You know, Jung can't calculate. When Choo's butterfly fingers dance over the abacus in front of her and he tells her that two baskets are missing, she has to believe him. Jung is like a mute who has swallowed bitter grass but is unable to voice it. It's a setup. Before Jung can argue with Choo all the people around her — the squid seller, the cigarette seller, and the liquor seller — act as witnesses for Mr. Choo. In one voice, they say that Jung is wrong. It is . . . as if they already knew the answer before Accountant Choo's fingers even touched the abacus . . . I need your help, Maple. I must figure this out."

It was eight o'clock in the evening. We found Jung sitting on her tricycle sobbing. She had been accused again. She was afraid of losing her job if the mysterious mistake kept repeating itself. Accountant Choo was firm that there had been no fault on his part. Jung's fellow fishermen were upset, but they were unable to prove Jung's innocence.

The baskets filled with seafood were distributed to each booth. The market employees came and began to sort the fish. I was hungry and wanted to go home. But Wild Ginger insisted that I stay. She was spying on Mr. Choo. She moved her stall toward the east corner where she could keep Choo in sight. She pretended that she was sharpening her scissors.

"It looks like he is getting ready to take off." Wild Ginger quickly pulled me to her side. "I want you to follow me, Maple. Keep at a distance but keep me in your sight."

"You're not going to do something dangerous, are you?"

"Of course not," Wild Ginger replied without looking at me. She quickly put down her scissors and closed her stall.

I watched Accountant Choo. He locked his abacus away in a cart and pushed the cart into a storage space next to a booth. Out he came carrying a black plastic bag. He crossed the street and entered a public restroom. After a short while he came out, followed by men with familiar faces. They were the discount seafood seller, the cigarette seller, and the liquor seller. They were pulling up their zippers and looking around at the same time. They walked separately but toward the same direction heading north. I backed a few yards from Wild Ginger and pretended that I was passing by.

The group of men formed a triangle with Accountant Choo at its head. After they passed the neighborhood they began to walk faster. We followed them across a construction site, a waste site, an abandoned plastic-tube factory, and onto the grounds of the cigarette factory, which seemed to be closed for the day. The doorman let the group in after he was thrown a pack of cigarettes.

"They are hitting the factory's storage area." Wild Ginger waved at me. Together we began circling the building. Finally we arrived at the back of the factory where tobacco was heaped high.

"How do you know?" I was watching Accountant Choo and his group disappear behind a wall.

"I have been following them but I have never gotten inside the storage area. I want to see what they are doing. Would you wait here?"

Before I could say anything Wild Ginger was gone. She had climbed the fence and leapt to the other side.

I was nervous. My stomach gnawed at me with fear. The sky was now very dark and Wild Ginger was nowhere to be seen. There was no light. The area looked so desolate that it seemed the perfect place for a crime. Suddenly Wild Ginger reappeared. She ran toward me but didn't cross the fence.

"Let's go," I urged.

"Maple, I want you to notify the police immediately."

"What?"

"They are distributing the money that they have stolen!"

"Are you sure, Wild Ginger?"

"Sure! Go now!"

"What about you?"

"I need to keep an eye on them."

"But —"

"Hurry!" She turned and ran back into the darkness.

I tried to envision what she would do. If they caught her they could murder her right here, easy, I thought.

I left quickly. For a moment I was disoriented, too nervous to recognize directions. Finally I managed to get back to my own neighborhood. I zipped through lanes and passed my own door. The light in my house was already off. My mother always shut the light off early in order to save electricity. I told myself to keep going until I arrived at the door of the neighborhood police guard. I knocked.

The guard opened the door. He was eating his dinner. His motorcycle was parked in the center of the room. Hearing my report he immediately phoned his headquarters. "The patrol is on the way." He wiped his oily mouth and put on his jacket. Starting his motorcycle he said, "Get on the back with me, kid."

By the time the police and the patrol arrived Wild Ginger's face was scratched and her right arm hung loose in front of her chest. Trying to stop Choo and his group from escaping she was almost strangled to death. The police chief arrested Choo and his group on the spot.

Wild Ginger was sent to the local hospital. Evergreen and I followed her into the large building. In an operating room, we sat by her side while doctors tended to her. They set her arm and wrapped it in a cast. They gave her blood transfusions and stitched up her cuts. I dampened her lips with a wet towel. She was in enormous pain. Evergreen offered his hand. She grabbed it and breathed deeply. I watched the sweat on her forehead turn into crystal beads. Evergreen kept talking to her, trying to distract her from the pain. It surprised me to see the usually quiet Evergreen chatting away like a young wide-eyed boy. He told Wild Ginger stories of his childhood, of his father's adventures as a sailor, his achievements and accidents, and later his strokes and nerve disorders. He told her how he and his late mother helped the old man when he was paralyzed. And finally about his own early dream of becoming a captain. He got excited when mentioning a toy ship he made when he was ten.

"It's giant." He spread out his arms to show its length. "It's got a hundred and twenty-three compartments. It took twenty pounds of wood and six hundred empty matchboxes. I had collected matchboxes since I was seven. The ship took me two years to complete. I named it *Victory.*"

Wild Ginger was quiet. She looked, no, stared at Evergreen, as if it weren't her body the doctor's needles were going through.

"I used to make rainbow soap papers as a child," she told Evergreen after she was sent to the recovery room. "I was fascinated with the process. I went door to door to collect soap scraps. I scrubbed the leftover soap from soap boxes. After I had a bucketful, I melted it on the stove. I added fragrant jasmine petals. Then I divided the paste in different bowls and dyed it different colors. I stirred the paste under the sun until it became thick. Then I took pieces of cardboard and cut them into all kinds of shapes. I coated the papers with the paste. After they dried the fragrance became strong. There was nothing else like them. You could take the papers anywhere and wash your hands with them. I liked them so much that I didn't use them. I put them in my Mao books. I looked at and smelled them every day when I worked on my reciting."

"You must show them to me."

"When you show me your wooden ship."

Wild Ginger was visited by the district party secretary in the hospital. Overnight she was pronounced a heroine and a revolutionary model. She was interviewed by the *People's Daily* and the *Liberation Daily*. The next morning her story was on every household's breakfast table. The journalists asked if Wild Ginger had been directed by Mao's teaching during her brave exploit. Not only did she give a positive answer, she provided the details in the paragraph of Mao's teaching which had inspired her action. Her words were printed with quotation marks and underlines. She was now a true champion.

I was thrilled for Wild Ginger. But in the meantime I wondered if reciting Mao at the moment of being strangled was possible. Maybe Mao was the driving force behind her action. Maybe she had become a true Maoist.

I was interviewed as well. But when asked what was on my mind when fetching the policeman, I said that I was thinking about Wild Ginger's safety.

"Are you sure that you didn't think of Mao's teaching?" the journalist asked. "For example, 'It's our duty to help our comrade . . .'?"

"No, not really."

"Not a bit?"

"Well, I lost my way and was trying to find it."

"No Mao thoughts?"

"I wish —"

"Which paragraph?"

"I can't remember."

"You have to be honest."

"Well, no then. I am sorry."

"Wild Ginger's mind had only Mao's teaching at that moment. Why don't you think clearly before giving me an answer?"

"I was . . . too scared to think."

"Fine." The journalist closed his notebook and stood up.

"But I helped." I felt wronged.

"Well, that is not significant enough material."

The newspapers printed photos of Wild Ginger with her right arm in a cast. Her smile was proud. The title said MAO'S TEACHING GUIDED OUR HEROINE TO VICTORY. Wild Ginger was brought to meet the general party secretary of Shanghai. The secretary was on his way to Beijing and he wanted to introduce Wild Ginger to Chairman Mao.

The news brought honor to the city, district, and neighborhood. Wild Ginger's coming meeting with Chairman Mao was the glory of everyone. The school held a big ceremony in Wild Ginger's name. Evergreen was called to give a speech on the heroine's hard work in studying Mao quotations. I was called the heroine's "comrade in arms" and was asked to comment on her life. In the meantime I was rewarded with a wok-size Mao button.

My parents got emotional when thinking of Mrs. Pei. Had Mrs. Pei been alive she would have been so happy. My mother went to Wild Ginger's house at night and burned incense beneath the fig tree.

Our former teacher, Mrs. Cheng, was in joyful tears when she came and chatted with my mother. "Wild Ginger inherited her mother's character."

"I can't agree with you more," Mother responded. "Mrs. Pei was honorably stubborn. She would rather have had her head removed than give up her feelings for Mr. Pei. But how could she have any idea how Wild Ginger would turn out?"

"'A piece of real gold fears no fire,'" recited Mrs. Cheng. "When Wild Ginger was brought to my class I knew she was talented and would sooner or later distinguish herself."

The fishwoman Jung was brought onto the stage to tell her story. "It doesn't surprise me that Chairman Mao wants to receive Wild Ginger," Jung said. "Wild Ginger is the best of all his disciples. Serving the people with heart and soul is exactly what Wild Ginger has been practicing."

Hot Pepper pushed herself through the crowd and was

trying to shake hands with the heroine. Wild Ginger paid no attention. She walked right past Hot Pepper to give an interview to a radio journalist. Her voice through the loudspeakers was resonant and filled with passion.

At the school gate, the general party secretary's jeep was waiting for Wild Ginger. The jeep was covered with red crepe-paper flowers. A crowd was cheering.

Wild Ginger emerged from the school principal's office in her uniform. She was surrounded by people. Before letting her get into the jeep the principal and the heads of the neighborhood and district competed to show their affection. They took off their own treasured Mao buttons and pinned them to Wild Ginger's clothes.

"Learn from our heroine, Wild Ginger!" Hot Pepper led the crowd to shout.

"Salute to our heroine, Wild Ginger!"

"Long live Chairman Mao!"

I followed the slogan and shouted. I thought of Hot Pepper's umbrella and Wild Ginger's broken abacus.

As a result of Wild Ginger's meeting with Chairman Mao a series of events took place.

First, our neighborhood committee put up a bulletin to notify all citizens that the late Mr. and Mrs. Pei's identities had been reevaluated. Instead of being called the "French spies," they were now to be called the "international Communists."

Second, a report of the conversation between Wild Ginger and Chairman Mao was nationally distributed. It read:

Wild Ginger: Chairman Mao, unfortunately I was born with a political defect. I am a quarter French.

Chairman Mao: The late Canadian doctor Norman Bethune was not a Chinese. But it didn't stop him from coming to China and participating in the Chinese revolution. It didn't stop him from opening a hospital to serve our Red Army. He died on duty, of a blood infection, but his spirit, his utter devotion to others without any thought of self, was shown in his work, in his warm-heartedness toward all comrades and people. We must all learn the spirit of absolute selflessness from him. One's background is irrelevant. One's performance counts and that is what makes one who he is. A man's ability may be great or small, but if he has this spirit, he is already noble-minded and pure, a man of moral integrity and above vulgar interest, a man who is of value to the people.

Wild Ginger: Dear Chairman, I thank you for the enlightenment.

Chairman Mao: Also, revolution is not only a Chinese subject. Karl Marx was not Chinese either. The Chinese revolution has inherited the great French Revolution's tradition. You should be proud that you have an internationalist's blood.

Wild Ginger: How should I continue to devote myself to your teaching?

Chairman Mao: Keep in mind that the duty to liberate the world rests on the shoulders of the young people.

Third, the whole neighborhood was mobilized to help remodel Wild Ginger's house. As a political project, the house was fixed in a week. The district party secretary personally came and rolled up his sleeves and trousers and worked on the walls.

Fourth, Wild Ginger was given not only a full scholarship for the rest of her school years but a monthly allowance as well. She was treated as an orphan of revolutionary martyrs and was granted a handsome martyr's pension.

Fifth, Wild Ginger was accepted as the youngest member of the Communist party and was pronounced the commander in chief of the Red Guard.

The day of Wild Ginger's return was made into a festival. A parade was designed to welcome her. From the airport the roads were crossed with banners. Hundreds and thousands of schoolchildren were lined up on each side of the road to greet her. The city's normal traffic was banned. The crowd extended throughout the city all the way to the east end — the bank of the Huangpu River.

I was given a big task — to be a human sculpture of the heroine. It was supposed to be the highlight of the parade. I stood twenty-five feet high, on top of a bus that had been converted into a stage. Behind me was a hundred-man drum team, all dressed in red silk gowns with their drumsticks tied with colorful silk strings. The drums were as large as backyard ponds.

I was dressed in a green army uniform tied with a belt at the waist. My hair was done in Wild Ginger's fashion: two short braids at the ears. I held a larger-than-life Mao Quotation Book made of cardboard. I was told to pose with my chest protruding and my head turned at a forty-five-degree angle. My right ankle was tied to a pole for stability. Under my feet were four boys on their hands and knees, posed as the villains. The one who wore dark-framed glasses was supposed to be Accountant Choo. The rest played the cigarette seller, the squid seller, and the liquor seller. Their faces were painted blue and purple while mine was powdered with red and pink. We were already sweating hard.

The bamboo poles supporting me swayed when there was wind. Although the bus driver drove slowly, it was still scary. I felt that I could be pitched into the air at any moment. The crowd cheered at the top of their lungs when they saw us pass. I tried to act as calmly as I could, but every time the bus made a jerky stop the poles bent to an impossible angle. I was so scared that I almost wet my pants. The boys beneath my feet begged me not to scream and promised that they would hold me. Gradually I got used to the sway. As our bus passed, the children cried, "Look! The heroine Wild Ginger! Wild Ginger!"

I was exhausted. The boys had abandoned their poses and came to lean on each other. As the poles swayed again I almost landed on the drummers' heads. When the poles swung back I let out a breath. The boys stuck out their thumbs to praise me — forgetting their roles as villains.

The sound of the drums shook the city. After the parade crossed Liberation Boulevard, I could see the riverfront.

Behind me the drum buses were followed by accordion bands, the red-flag holders, and the sunflower dancers.

"Split the lines and yield to the side!" came the general party secretary's order, which was passed down through an electrical amplifier. "Let the heroine through!"

"Welcome home! The biggest welcome!" the crowd cheered.

To my excitement, a green jeep led by three motorcycles appeared.

Wild Ginger stood in the open jeep waving at the crowd. Next to her were four armed soldiers. She was in a full new army outfit with a red-star cap on her head. She was shining and gloriously beautiful.

Could she see me? Did she know that I was playing her? I clapped my hands so hard that my palms began to hurt. It didn't feel real. It felt like a dream.

Her new house was ordered to be completed the day before her return. Her favorite Mao quotations were copied onto the walls by the best calligrapher in the country. The roof edges were laid with ceramic tiles of sunflowers. The house stood out like a glistening castle among bleak rocks.

Would she miss her mother in the new house?

12

She was ahead of me. We had been apart for only a month but she seemed to have grown much taller than I. Her sunlit eyes were brighter than ever. She stood in a new pair of green army boots. We chatted endlessly, walking from her house to my house and then back to hers. Finally, we settled ourselves under the fig tree and carried the conversation into the night.

"You won't believe it, Maple. I am troubled." Her tune suddenly changed.

"Sure, you can't stand your luck."

"Seriously, I need your advice."

"Tell me, is it the frostbite that's bothering you?"

"Something terribly wrong has come between me and Evergreen."

"The last thing I knew about you two was you showed him your soap-paper collection and he showed you the wooden ship."

"That's exactly when it happened."

"What? What happened?"

"It's . . . how shall I put it . . . unhealthy."

"Unhealthy?"

"We were in my house."

"Yes?"

"No one was around."

"Yes?"

"You are sixteen."

"And he is eighteen. What are you afraid of?"

"Well," she sighed in frustration, "you don't understand."

"Well, talk to me."

"I don't know."

"You think I am an idiot."

"It's confusing."

"Did . . . did he . . . ?" I didn't want to think in that direction.

"No, of course not. How could we . . . we are both Maoists!"

"Then what's the problem?"

"It's . . . me. I wanted to . . . I . . . well, it's awful, bizarre and fantastic at the same time."

"What did you do?"

"Nothing."

"So?"

"It's happening inside, in my head, everything changed from that moment on."

"I'm getting it."

"After we showed each other the collection and ran out of things to say, it was odd. We suddenly became awkward. He said that he must get going but he didn't move. I said goodbye, but my heart prayed for him to ask me to stay."

"Why didn't you talk about Chairman Mao? You love to talk about Chairman Mao."

"I was out of myself. I was not the same person I knew."

"I see."

"My eyes were eating him up. It was . . . as if I were seduced. I could feel it coming, trying to pull me down to the water."

"What about him?"

"He stared at me like a criminal who heard his death sentence."

"What time was it?"

"I don't remember. It was getting dark. I was kind of afraid of myself. I felt I was going crazy. Because I wanted —"

"What?"

"I wanted him . . . I wanted to have his lips on my mouth."

I stared at her.

"Shocking, isn't it?" she asked after seeing that I wouldn't or couldn't respond. "It was dreadful. Almost helpless. I couldn't stop myself. I knew it was not right. I am a Maoist. A model for the youth. I have promised the party and myself to be pure. But here I was, throwing my honor away, committing myself to a temptation."

"I envy you."

"Maple, what kind of nonsense are you uttering?"

"Our bodies are going to do what's natural."

Her expression changed. "Please stop it. You talk like a reactionary."

"Come on, Wild Ginger. You don't have to be on duty in front of me. I know who you are."

"You don't, really."

"Come on."

"I mean it."

I went quiet and turned away.

"Please, Maple."

"I can't tell you what you want to hear."

"Then don't."

"But I disagree with you."

"Everyone has to be guided by the principles of Chairman Mao."

"What about private matters? What about intimacy where you place trust in someone who will in turn guard it with honor?"

"Such intimacy doesn't exist in the world of the true proletarians. The rule is: we live for one thing, to serve and sacrifice for Chairman Mao."

"So you don't acknowledge love."

"That is a bourgeois word. You should delete it from your vocabulary."

We were standing by the garbage dump where Wild Ginger had stabbed her hand once. It seemed a safe place to carry on our discussion, where no one would be able to hear us.

The late autumn leaves were blown by the wind and danced in the air. In sandals, my bare feet were getting cold. To keep them warm, I crunched the leaves and hopped once in a while. Our discussion was going nowhere. We fought, trying not to raise our voices. I was surprised to learn that while she was in Beijing she had sworn her loyalty by writing a letter of promise. The idea was generated by the secretary in chief of the National Communist Youth League. The letter stated that she would give up her personal life, including marriage, to be a people's servant and a Maoist. The People's House of Letters and Literature had given her a contract to publish her diary of the next ten years. The text would be included in school textbooks and recited by students at all levels.

"It's such an honor that I was set to be an immortal," she said.

I asked if she believed that this was the right thing to do.

"No doubt I do," she answered.

"What about Evergreen?"

"I'll overcome my feelings for him."

"You mean you won't —"

"We are revolutionary soulmates."

"No, I mean, will you ever become . . . involved?"

"You mean like —"

"I mean like . . . lovers."

"Never."

"You expect me to believe you?"

"Chairman Mao teaches us, 'A true Communist is one who keeps her word.'"

"What do you want me to say?"

"Be proud of me."

"I am. But I also feel sad."

"Why?"

"I can't imagine your life being companionless. It'll be lonely."

"Loneliness doesn't belong to a Maoist. Don't you see I have people? I have one billion people loving me and looking up to me."

"You are missing my point."

"Grow up, Maple."

"You . . . you don't want to be with Evergreen, is that right?"

"Wrong."

"I don't get it."

"I'll be with him. We will spend a great deal of time, even our lives, together, but without any physical contact."

"Without any?"

She nodded, in full confidence.

"What about Evergreen? Will he accept your condition?"

"He has to, if he is what he says . . . if he cares about me."

"What if he discovers that love has to be expressed beyond spirituality?"

"Then he has to go."

"Would you let him?"

"Like I said, my loyalty toward Chairman Mao comes first."

"What about your desire?"

"That's where I need you, Maple. I am determined to fight the beast inside me and win. It will be hard at the beginning, but I'll pull through. Evergreen and I will get used to being with each other like —"

"A brother and a sister?" My tone was ironic.

She didn't mind. "We will have to work on reforming our thinking. Any bad thought will be nipped in the bud. We will conquer ourselves and then the world."

"What about impulse?"

"You'll be the one to help me to hold the leash."

"Well, I'll do my best to help, but —"

"You'll be all right."

"Describe my duty."

"Just be there."

"Be where?"

"Be where we are."

"We? You mean you and Evergreen? You want me to be a big bright bulb hanging in between you and him —"

"Exactly. With your presence, my instinct will be caged."

"But Evergreen will throw me out!"

"He won't know that you're there."

"What do you mean?"

"I'll hide you."

"Where?"

"In the closet."

13

After dinner she hurried me into her closet, which stood in the middle of a long wall. She had rearranged its colored glass panes so I could peek through without being seen. The closet was originally a living room fireplace. The remodeling knocked down the bedroom walls and turned the whole house into one big space. There were sets of red panels elegantly calligraphed with Mao poems. Wild Ginger said that these would be used to divide future Mao study groups into small discussions. The living area occupied a quarter of the space. Her bed was on its left, kitchen on the right, and her dining table with a set of benches was in the middle.

We were waiting for Evergreen.

"It's such a relief to think that there will be a real skeleton in the closet," she said excitedly. "I feel that I am protected." She was full of spirit. She wore a clean white cotton shirt with red plum flowers around the collar. Her developing chest made the shirt look tight. She had been using the smallest-size bra. I thought, She doesn't have a Chinese body.

"Are you all set?" Her voice was charged. "He could be here any minute."

I had mixed feelings about doing this. I didn't feel comfortable spying on Evergreen. Reason one was that I respected him. Reason two was that I was, to be frank, jealous. Although I hadn't had the good fortune to attract Evergreen's attention, I was not without feelings toward him, so I felt awkward watching him pursue Wild Ginger.

Yet I couldn't say no to her. The moment she rescued me from Hot Pepper's umbrella, I was determined to repay her kindness. To lend her a hand when she needed it was my duty. And I wanted to protect her.

Finally there came a light knock on the door. Evergreen showed up with a Mao book under his arm. A comrade handshake. They both looked uneasy. "Make yourself comfortable," she said and walked away to fetch him water. He stared at her new soft-soled black sandals. A skillful shoemaker, she had made them herself. I made crooked shoes. My biggest problem was that when I stitched the sole and top together, the right shoe always ended up looking like a poorly wrapped wonton. I had to hammer the shoe to get it to match the other.

Evergreen settled down on the bench. He was wearing

slacks and a blue sweatshirt with the number 8 on the front. On the back was THE GREAT WALL CLIMBER. He wore a pair of white tennis shoes.

"Have you eaten?" he asked Wild Ginger almost nervously.

"I've eaten," she replied, flushing.

He scratched his head, then wiped his brow.

She sat down on a bench across from him. "Shall we start?"

He nodded, opening the Mao book.

"By the way, what do you think of the place?" she asked, flipping the pages of the book.

"Neat. It reminds me of the warehouse where my father used to work. I like the space."

"I ordered the four walls painted deep red, did you notice?" she said proudly. "I did the Mao portraits myself. They aren't perfect but they're from my heart. I intend to make the space an ongoing Mao exhibition."

"Well, you have it." He got up to admire the calligraphy of Mao poems.

"Be careful with the statue," she warned as he turned. Toward the entrance there stood a life-size glow-in-the-dark Mao sculpture, its right hand waving above the head in the air.

"Does it really glow at night?"

"It comes alive."

"I can see you talking to him."

"I do."

He went back to sit down. He looked at Mrs. Pei's old

clock on the wall, which had been damaged by one of the Red Guards during the looting. After Wild Ginger's meeting with Chairman Mao, the district party secretary was personally ordered to locate the clock and bring it back to Wild Ginger fixed.

"This is really fancy!" Evergreen pointed at the gas stove. "What a luxury!" He played with the knob and was amazed to see it work. "You never have to visit the filthy coal shop and carry the heavy loads again. Your mother would have enjoyed it if she had lived."

"She would." Wild Ginger lowered her head and looked at the plants on the floor. The camellias, red grass, orchids, and thick-leaved bamboo — all Mrs. Pei's favorites.

"'To be good at translating the party's policy into action of the masses, to be good at getting not only the leading cadres but also the broad masses to understand and master every movement and every struggle we launch — this is the art of Marxist-Leninist leadership. It is also the dividing line that determines whether or not we make mistakes in our work . . .'"

They were taking turns reading Mao's paragraphs. Next was Evergreen's turn. He had a great voice, and his Mandarin was perfect. "'. . . However active the leading group may be, its activity will amount to a fruitless effort by a handful of people unless combined with the activity of the masses. On the other hand, if the masses alone are active without a strong leading group to organize their activity properly, such activity cannot be sustained for long, or carried forward in the right direction, or raised to a high level."

Wild Ginger took over again. "'Production by the masses, the interests of the masses, the experiences and the feelings of the masses — to these the leading cadres should not only pay attention but great focus . . .'"

I wished that I could be more interested in the content. Bored, I waited impatiently for their break.

Finally, after the clock struck ten, there was the sound of a movement.

I glued my eye to the peephole. And I saw Evergreen put down his Mao book.

Wild Ginger raised her head.

They stared at each other.

Evergreen picked up the cup and drank down the water. "Page five hundred four, paragraph three. Ready? Begin." He read almost angrily, "'Communists must be ready at all times to stand up for the truth . . .'"

She looked distracted but followed the reading, "'. . . because truth is in the interests of the people . . . Communists must be ready at all times . . .'" He suddenly got up, then sat down frustratedly. "'. . . to correct their mistakes, because . . .'"

"'. . . mistakes are against the interest of the people.'" She took a deep breath.

He stopped turning the page.

She closed the book.

He looked at her.

She turned her face away.

"I have to go," he uttered, standing up.

"One more paragraph," she said. "We must meet our day's goal."

He sat back down.

"Page five hundred six, paragraph three, Chairman Mao teaches us . . ."

"'Communists must always go into the whys and wherefores of anything,'" he recited. "'They must use their own heads and carefully think over whether or not it corresponds to reality and is really well founded . . .'"

She stole a glance at him, then continued, "'. . . On no account should they follow blindly —'"

At that he rose and rushed toward the hallway. Without saying goodbye he ran out and slammed the door behind him.

Wild Ginger sat still like the clock on the wall.

"Thank you, it's a success," she said weakly.

"Do you wish that he had stayed?"

She turned to me and recited, "'Provoking positive thoughts is just as important as battling the negative. Encouraging sentimentality is just as bad as selling national secrets to the enemy.'"

I detected tears behind her voice.

That night I went home and asked my mother about men for the first time.

"Shame on you," was Mother's reply. "Why don't you

think of something better to do? We're out of food again. Why don't you go to the market with your brothers and sisters and pick some leaves from the trash bin?"

"It's afternoon, the edible leaves are long gone." I felt depressed.

"Well, try to go early in the morning while everybody is still asleep."

Wild Ginger and Evergreen had been practicing the same ritual for three weeks now. They sat head to head and acted like poorly made puppets whose movements were stiff. They didn't even say hello to each other when Evergreen arrived on the last day. The experience of being together seemed to offer no joy, yet neither of them called it quits. It was as if they were catering to an addiction.

I was getting sick of the closet. I was losing patience. In the dark, my thoughts raced. My mind was a jar of marinated pictures. Pictures of unrelated events, past and present blending into each other. Pictures of my swelling imagination, which produced horrifying results. I became obsessed with what could happen and was determined to stay in the closet until I saw "it."

I couldn't pinpoint when my focus began to change. I peeped through the hole one night and realized that I had been looking at Evergreen. I was examining him, in the most disgusting way: I memorized the number of pimples on his face, their location and size, how they changed day by day, and how his old skin flaked and grew new skin. I paid attention to the shape of his wide shoulders, big hands, and thick fingers. I indulged in the movement of his lips. My ears picked out his voice from their duets. Something rotten was infesting my insides.

I told Wild Ginger that I would like to quit.

"I'd call it a betrayal if you dare." Displeased, she threatened to terminate our friendship.

I pleaded, almost begging.

Wild Ginger held my hands with great concern. "Let's talk."

I shook my head. "You must release me from this before something terrible happens."

She laughed. "You are just bored."

"Let's take a break," Wild Ginger said at nine o'clock. She looked at Evergreen. There were butterflies in her smile.

Evergreen had acted oddly since his arrival. He had been struggling with himself from the moment he sat down. He kept changing his sitting position. "Have we read enough?" he finally asked.

She avoided his eyes. "Would you like to have some tea?"

He got up and followed her to the stove. She lit a match and put on the pot.

Standing behind her, he examined the stove.

"Try it." She turned the gas off and threw him the matchbox.

He lit the match.

She turned on the gas. "Now!"

He reached out.

The flame ring looked like a blue necklace.

He turned to her with the match still burning between his fingers.

"Whooo!" She bent over and blew. "Are you thinking about burning my hair?"

They were inches away from each other.

His hands went out, as if by themselves.

She was held, her head, her neck.

He held the pose in shock, didn't dare to move.

She struggled, but didn't run away.

He bent down toward her lips.

Her mind seemed to halt.

He let his mouth fall.

My heart raced.

Gradually their kisses turned into a wrestling match.

His hands went to free himself from his clothes.

He moved her toward the kitchen counter.

His clothes began to fall on the floor piece by piece. First the jacket, then the shirt. His chest was now bare.

Her will seemed to be paralyzed. She let him wrap her with his arms.

Pushing her against the corner of the wall he rocked himself against her.

My chest swelled.

There was no air in the closet.

My sweat steamed. I tried to hold my breath and tried not to blink.

I saw his hand reaching down to his zipper.

The pants peeled off like banana skin.

His butt was dark brown, tightly muscled. It reminded me of a horse's.

"Evergreen," Wild Ginger cried.

He didn't answer. He got down on his knees, pressing her onto the floor.

"Evergreen!"

He reached one arm out, lifted her, and spread his jacket beneath her. In one motion he laid himself on top of her and began caressing her.

I was completely rapt.

Wild Ginger cried. I couldn't identify whether it was from pain or pleasure.

His hands unbuttoned her shirt. Her breasts popped out, and he threw himself onto them.

"No!" she screamed as if waking up from a dream.

He locked her back into his arms.

"No!" she repeated, pushing him away. Then she sat up and looked in my direction.

He seemed confused. He followed her stare toward the closet.

I became nervous. In a hurry to pull myself away from the peephole I accidentally knocked down a tiny piece of decorative wood frame.

"What is it?" He was alarmed.

"My neighbor's cat." She turned him away. "It likes to visit the closet."

The night ended. Evergreen went home frustrated. I came out of the closet exhausted. Wild Ginger thanked me. She was proud of herself and promised that she would not be needing me much longer.

I felt somehow manipulated and said that I would like to go home.

"You don't want to chat?" Her cheeks were rosy red. She was stunningly beautiful. "You don't want to know what I feel? You saw everything, didn't you?"

"It's kind of late."

"Your mother knows that you're at my house." She followed me to the door.

"So how do you feel?" I stopped and turned around.

She didn't seem to detect my emotion. "I almost regretted that I signed that letter to give up my personal life."

"You two . . . fit."

"What do you mean?"

"You make a good pair."

"He possesses a strange power. It is hard for me to fight it. He almost made me drink poison."

"Would you?"

She smiled. It was splendid. "I have made my commitment — Chairman Mao comes first."

"Then why do you fool around?"

"I wish I knew the answer. Part of me just can't resist Evergreen. I know I'm playing with fire. But I'm on guard. I have you, the fire extinguisher, on hand."

I wanted to point out that she was selfish, but instead I said flatly, "It was quite educational."

She giggled. "Was it your first time seeing a man's body?"

"A woman's body too, besides my own."

"That . . . thing, his instrument, is rather ugly, isn't it?"

I stood up, feeling uncomfortable. "I must leave now, Wild Ginger."

"May I count on you next time Evergreen is here?"

I tried to gather my courage to reject her.

"Oh, please." She threw herself at me, arms wrapped around my neck. "I have no one else."

"It'll be the last time."

"All right, the last time."

I was reluctant to get up the next day. I felt dispirited. Thankfully, it was Sunday. I stayed in bed until noon. My mother thought that I was coming down with something. She sent my sister Erh-Mei to the market to buy ginger so she could make soup for me. It took Erh-Mei a long time to get back.

"What took so long?" Mother asked her in a whisper, assuming that I was asleep.

"There was a parade," Erh-Mei reported.

"Don't tell me the Red Guards are trying to teach the zoo dance again."

"That is exactly what's going on. By the way, Mama, it's *Zhong* dance. 'Zhong,' for loyalty, not 'zoo.' You can get yourself in serious trouble if you mispronounce the word. They will name you a reactionary and treat you like Mrs. Pei."

"Well, I just won't say that word again."

"I am afraid that you have to. The Zhong dance instructors are coming to teach in this neighborhood this week. Everyone has to show up. It's a public service you must attend. It's going to take up the whole week. The bosses at your work units have already been notified. All the workers will be given the work time to participate in the dance."

"I'll take the time to sneak home," Mother said.

"No, you will be punished if you do that," Erh-Mei warned. "There will be a performance at the end of the learning session. If you don't pass, your loyalty toward Chairman Mao will be questioned."

"But I can't dance! I have never danced in my life!"

"It's not a matter of can or can't dance. It's a matter of showing loyalty toward Chairman Mao. It's a matter of showing that all the people in the neighborhood are mobilized. We sing in one voice and dance in one style. It's a political demonstration to our enemies domestic and international. There is a competition among districts, and the instructors are already feeling very pressured."

"Who are these people anyway?"

"The Maoists."

"Well, to teach me to dance would be like teaching a mute to sing."

"You are lucky, Mama. The instructors are Maple's best friends, Wild Ginger and Evergreen. They'll let you take all the time you need. It might be fun."

"Yeah. And my old face will have no place to hide. Just to think about it shortens my life."

"If you are really embarrassed, there is a trick. You can ask to play the sunflower. That way, your face will always be behind the flower head."

I didn't feel any better after the ginger soup, so I decided to take a walk. Throwing on my jacket, I went out the door. After a few blocks I turned into Red Sun Park. The mid-March weather was warm. The park was full of pink peach blossoms, thick and cloudlike. The ground was carpeted with petals.

I lay down on a bench. Petals gently snowed down on my face. The sun's rays streamed through the branches. To avoid the sun, I turned my face to the side toward a bamboo pavilion. To my surprise, I saw a familiar figure sitting inside. I sat up to make sure. "Evergreen!" My voice betrayed me.

It *was* he. He waved. He was in the same blue sportswear.

"Don't tell me you are zoo dancing here!" I tried to be funny. I didn't know what else to say. I didn't know if I should move toward him or back out of the park. I thought about his naked back, his firm buttocks. I got up to walk toward him, but my feet became tangled. I felt that he somehow knew I had spied on him.

"Oh, I am taking a break here." He stood up to greet me. "I am tired of teaching the dances."

"Why don't you do that at home?" I decided just to stay where I was. We stood about fifteen feet away from each other. The distance was awkward for conversation but it comforted me.

"Well, I'm drafted constantly from my house."

"You mean Wild Ginger?"

He laughed. "No one escapes her."

I tried to figure out the meaning between his lines.

"You look deadly serious, Maple, like a party secretary. Come over, sit down. Let's have a chat, please."

"I . . ." I looked around as if trying to find a clock. "I'm late. I have to get going."

"Where?"

"A . . . drugstore. My mother is waiting for me."

"If you are in such a hurry, why did you even come to the park?"

I lost the courage to keep lying. "All right, I am not in a hurry."

"Come on, I haven't seen you for a long time. You must tell me how you have been and you might be curious about how I've been."

I saw you, heard you, and talked about you almost daily, my mind's voice said.

"Tell me something, talk to me, Maple," he said, looking at me.

The image of his naked body kept surfacing in front of my eyes.

"I've been doing fine," I said dryly.

"Have you been with Wild Ginger lately?"

I went silent.

"I am sure you have," he concluded. "You are each other's shadows. Did she . . . does she confide in you?"

"Sort of."

"Did she tell you anything . . . about me?"

"I don't know. I . . . am not sure . . . Well, I don't think so."

"I need a favor, Maple," he said.

"I am listening."

"It might not make sense to you, but I am experiencing something I'd like to try to share with you. Well, are you ready? Chairman Mao . . . All right, are you with me? Let me know if I lose you —"

"I am not sure if I want to hear it, Evergreen."

"I'll make it short. Very short. Gee, this is not easy. The Chairman teaches us to be selfless. But I am discovering the self, myself really, as a human being. For the first time, I've started to see things through my own eyes instead of Chairman Mao's . . . It's devastating. My whole world is upside down now . . . It's puzzling to you, isn't it?"

"Well, when did you start to change? What happened?"

"The moment you brought Wild Ginger to me. I have discovered something more meaningful than preaching Maoism, something more satisfactory to my nature. Do you know how difficult it is for me to bring this up?"

"You aren't talking about abandoning Maoism, are you?"

"Indeed, that might be exactly the question."

"And it is a very dangerous one too."

"But no, it's not the issue of safety. I know I can trust you. I do trust you — it doesn't make sense but it's true that I feel I can trust you more than I can trust Wild Ginger. It might sound strange. She is a Mao zealot. Her loyalty is beyond reproach. Her eyes see only what's red. You are different. Your eyes reflect the rainbow. Now the risky part is, wait a minute, what do people do with the brain's waste?"

"What do you mean?"

"Give it a try. Your mind is always a step ahead of mine."

"I could have said something else."

"No, I appreciated your frankness." He paused for a while. His hands went into his pockets as if they were cold. Suddenly he asked, "What's Wild Ginger's decision? Can she . . . does she want to . . . I mean, does she feel the same way I do?"

My mind struggled. I had the answer but I didn't know how to give it. I couldn't say, Yes, Wild Ginger is attracted to you, but you are not worthy enough for her to break her vow to Chairman Mao.

"I'm not in any position to judge my friend," I finally uttered.

"Do you know that she showed me her diary?" He began walking.

"No." I followed him.

"Do you know she carries a diary?"

I made no reply because I couldn't say, It's a fake diary.

"We're" — he lowered his voice — "we are in each

other's lives at the moment. But I am puzzled by the way she acts."

"Are you or are you not in the diary?" I asked.

"No, I am not."

"It doesn't mean that you are not in her thoughts."

"Thank you. That's what I have been trying to tell my-self."

"The diary" — I don't know why I suddenly decided to blow this — "is for show. It's going to be published nation-wide and printed in textbooks."

"Then why the hell does she write it and call it a diary?"

"She is the Maoist model for the country. She has to do what's expected of a Maoist."

"This really bothers me. Maple, let me tell you some-thing. There is a wonderful part of her character and there is also a phony part. This is what we have been fighting: she wants no other life besides promoting Maoism. Her in-stincts might want what a human being wants but not her head. She's trying to kill off her human self."

"Well, you must understand that it is not easy to give up one's personal life for a national cause."

"National cause? Are you sincere, Maple?"

I found my defense weak — what bothered Evergreen bothered me too.

"I am not interested in teaching the zoo dancing at all, to tell you the truth."

"Aren't you supposed to say Zhong dancing?"

"I did it on purpose. To me it *is* zoo dancing — everyone has been forced into a barn. People have better things to do, like resting, taking care of their households, being together, cooking, reading, playing, and making —" He cut his words short and lowered his head.

"The first installment of her diary will be out in a couple of months." I brought back the subject.

"I won't read it," he said firmly, then asked, "Will you?"

"I might not enjoy it. But I will read it. I do everything she asks of me."

He turned to look at me suspiciously, then smiled. "You make me want to be a woman so I can get closer to Wild Ginger."

"I don't really feel close to her or even understand her."

"How do you mean?"

"This diary thing, for example. To publish it is to publish and legalize a big lie. It's harmful. It's dishonest. It'll damage the minds of the young. It's a false portrait of a Maoist. Not only will Wild Ginger suffer the consequences, other people will be forced to copy her — the model can do it, why can't you?"

"I shake hands with you, Maple. I shake hands with you. I really do. Thank you for answering my question . . . Wild Ginger is lucky to have a friend like you."

"Not necessarily." Somehow his compliments made me feel bitter. "She is lucky for what she has. It has nothing to do with me. She and I . . . I cannot achieve what she has achieved or is capable of achieving in the future. It's not that I agree with everything she does. I can't make myself be such an ardent Maoist. I'm not that driven. I am not that interested, or obsessed. I can recite a lot of quotations, though. It was a way to earn my place in the school and society. Wild Ginger is . . . I can't really say that she is being dishonest. Let's put it this way: she knows what it is like to be called an anti-Maoist. I won't question her motives. She writes the diary with sincerity. The reason she won't expose parts of herself is because she really believes that her behavior was immoral, and she is determined to fight it. She believes that she can overcome it."

"Will she?"

"She lives to win."

"Will there be a chance that someone might change her mind?"

"I'm not a good person to ask."

"Have you been encouraging her to be a Maoist?"

"No."

"Why?"

"I feel . . . sad, really sad. She has to give up so much to achieve her goal."

14

"Get up and attend the Zhong dancing class!" A group of neighborhood activists rang handbells throughout the lanes. "Order from the district party secretary!" "Ten o'clock, check yourself in at the marketplace!" "Show your loyalty toward Chairman Mao through your action!"

"Zoo class! Zoo class!" The children ran after the group and shouted cheerfully.

After the group made their rounds through the neighborhood, they came to knock on doors to make sure that everyone was out.

"Mama, time to go!" my sisters called. "The activists are knocking our door off its hinges."

"I'm trying to find my shoes! I can't go with slippers, can I?"

"Hurry up!"

"Zoo class!" Mother finally found her shoes. "Forcing an

old dog to catch a mouse. Buddha with your eyes open above."

Down the lane, One-Eye Grandpa greeted Mother. He was in baggy clothes. "I'm ready to have fun," he said to her. "Think of it this way, the dance will get your blood circulation going and boost your longevity." They chatted and Mother laughed in embarrassment.

The crowd grew thicker. There were hundreds of people, grouped in families, making their way to the market. We all wore blue or gray Mao jackets. Most of my neighbors were in their wooden slippers. *Tic, tac, tic, tac.* The noise was loud and pleasant to the ears.

Mother asked One-Eye Grandpa if he had ever danced before. The old man replied, "I studied traditional healing dance when I was young." He stopped and squatted down to demonstrate. After making some turns he started to hop on his feet like a frog. We all laughed and copied One-Eye Grandpa's hopping.

Finally we arrived at the market. The loudspeaker was broadcasting "We Can't Sail without Chairman Mao as a Helmsman." Although the song was much distorted, I still recognized the voice. It was Wild Ginger's. I could never forget her voice after she sang the French songs in the wheat field. This time she sang with energy and encouraged people to join her.

It was ten o'clock. The morning market had already been cleared up. The ground had been swept and washed, but the stinky smell was still there. The street was blocked by the activists and the emptied booths now filled with children. The neighbors lined up on one side of the street like cornstalks in a field. The line extended about a half mile.

Two loudspeakers were hung from a tree. Three accordions and four drums were playing. A man with his back facing us was conducting. It was Evergreen. He let the band rest whenever he could.

In the center of the stage stood Wild Ginger. She kept waving at Evergreen, asking him to keep the band playing. She was in her army uniform and the red-star cap with all her hair tucked in. She could be mistaken for a man if not for her full chest. "Chairman Mao teaches us, 'For hundreds of years the scholars had moved away from the people, and I began to dream of a time when the scholars would teach the coolies, for surely the coolies deserve teaching as much as the rest.' Now, let's put our great teacher's words into action! One, two, three, and four!" She instructed the neighbors to follow her steps. It was not easy. The old people like my mother just flung their arms and kicked their feet side to side. It was obvious that they were not interested in learning the dance. They were trying to kill time until they were released.

My mother was having difficulty. She asked Wild Ginger about being a sunflower.

"We won't have any costumes or props until the final recital."

So Mother was stuck. It didn't take long for her to relax — she saw other women who danced just as poorly.

They paid no attention to the music. No matter how many times Wild Ginger demonstrated the combo, they couldn't get it. I was sure that they were looking to be dismissed. But Wild Ginger was outrageously patient.

She sang and danced, demonstrating over and over again:

> The Yangtze River roared toward the East,
> The flower heads chased the red sun.
> Enthusiastically we dance and sing to you,
> Our great helmsman, Chairman Mao.
> We wish a long life,
> A long, long life to you.

Mother and her lady friends began to enjoy themselves. They chatted whenever Wild Ginger left them alone to practice. They moved their arms back and forth like brooms in sweeping motion. One woman was giving out a recipe. "I brew my own bean sprouts." She grapevined her legs. "The trick is that you have to put a wet cloth over the soaked beans to keep the basket moist at all times. And you put it in a straw rice warmer at night to keep up the temperature."

Mother was very interested. She copied the woman and twisted her legs from side to side. "I failed a couple of times trying to brew my own bean sprouts." She twisted her shoulders. "I'll try again, keeping your advice in mind."

"It saves you a lot of money if you figure out how to do it. It is the cheapest way to provide protein for your kids."

"Here, attention, everybody," Wild Ginger called. "'Enthusiastically we dance and sing to you, our great helmsman, Chairman Mao.' You must really show your expression! Like this, watch me! Like this, smile!"

Mother showed her teeth and quickened her steps.

"Do you know shortages are coming?" The woman put a hand over her mouth and bent toward Mother. "The government is running out of oil, salt, and matches. My son told me — he works for the national storage department. The warehouses have been emptied to keep the supply line alive to poor countries like Vietnam and Tanzania. We are drained but we can't afford to lose face. Chairman Mao has to look good to the world. But the soil doesn't understand this. It doesn't produce more just because we need it."

Mother shook her head, moving her limbs absent-mindedly.

"It's going to be terrible," the woman went on. "I have been stocking up."

"I have no use for my coupons, because I don't have money. It takes money to spend the coupons, you see, big sister," Mother said worriedly. "It's not that I don't need it. I need it badly. I have six kids. Six bottomless wells to fill. Seven ounces of oil per person per month has never been enough, yet I can't even afford to spend the oil coupons. We eat rice with plain salt, but still —"

"I have a trick for you, big sister . . ."

"You!" Wild Ginger's patience finally ran out. She pointed at the woman. "You have been talking since you got here. Not only do you show no loyalty to Chairman

Mao, you have been distracting others! Would you like to be sent to a mind-brushing school?"

"I'm terribly sorry!" The woman quickly moved away from my mother.

But Mother was not ready to give up the conversation. She was eager to learn the trick about stocking up. She tried to get closer to the woman.

"Attention!" Wild Ginger yelled loudly. "Now we are coming to the end of the dance. We are making a shiplike form. We will have the front with One-Eye Grandpa holding the national flag, the back with all of us holding Mao books, and a 'smokestack' in the middle with a Mao picture held high." She began to make arrangements by moving people around. "Listen, everyone has to fit into the formation."

My mother's friend was placed to be a "frame" of a "Mao picture holder." She and another woman were instructed to bend their knees to form a "ladder."

"We need someone to get up on their knees to hold the Mao picture." Wild Ginger turned to the crowd.

"How about me?" Mother volunteered. She must have seen the possibility of hiding her face behind the picture.

Wild Ginger hesitated.

"I am light," Mother added. "I'd like to show my loyalty toward our great leader by holding his very picture!"

"Are your limbs strong enough?"

"Chairman Mao's teaching will certainly strengthen me."

I was surprised at Mother's quick wit.

"Wonderful, aunt! You've got the job!"

Before Wild Ginger gave the instruction, Mother climbed on the "ladder."

Evergreen came and passed Mother the Mao picture. "Be careful, aunt!" He turned around and told the two women who were holding my mother's legs to keep her still. "Stabilize yourselves first. Let her down once she gets up there."

"No," Wild Ginger corrected him, "the pose has to be held for at least forty seconds so the stage will seem to freeze. That's how we'll make the most powerful impression!"

"You've got the right soldier for the task," Mother yelled.

"Move on." Wild Ginger went to arrange the other parts of the "ship."

"So what's the trick, big sister?" Mother finally resumed the conversation.

With her knees and arms trembling trying to hold my mother, the woman replied as her breath shortened, "Secretly sell your coupons to village dealers. They come to the city once a month to exchange sesame oil, salt, and matches for rice coupons and cotton coupons and oil coupons."

"But when exactly will they be coming next time? How will I find them?"

"Is everybody ready?" came Wild Ginger's call. "Let's practice. Ready? One, two, and three, begin! 'Enthusiastically we dance and sing to you, our great helmsman, Chairman Mao!'"

The crowd sang.

The drums beat loudly.

The accordion players worked their bellows as hard as they could.

"The fourth Tuesday of the month!" The woman's knee began to tremble so violently that Mother's knee almost buckled. "Six-thirty at the corner of Chia Chia Lane."

"I'll be there!" Mother said excitedly. It was followed by a deep sigh. "The reason I keep the coupons is because I hope that one day I'll be able to spend them. To buy cloth I need those coupons. All my bedsheets are worn out. My children dress like beggars."

"You'd better make use of those coupons before they expire."

"Will I get caught if I am seen?"

"Do it so that you won't get caught, big sister!" the woman gasped. "I've . . . never . . . gotten caught. Gee, this is torture."

The Mao picture in my mother's hands shook. "Thank you!" came Mother's voice from behind the frame.

"Oh, Buddha Heaven! I can't . . ." The woman's knee gave in.

"A long life to you! A long, long life to you!" the chorus sang.

Bang!

The Mao picture fell.

The "smokestack" collapsed.

The "ship" fell apart.

15

"'The masses have a potentially inexhaustible enthusiasm for socialism.'" Wild Ginger and Evergreen resumed their Mao study. "'Those who can only follow the old routine in a revolutionary period are utterly incapable of seeing this enthusiasm. They are blind and all is dark ahead of them. At times they go so far as to confound right and wrong and turn things upside down. Haven't we come across enough persons of this type?'"

It was eight o'clock at night. I was in the closet. Wild Ginger's voice was tired. She had been working to teach the Zhong dance for days without a stop. She slept four hours a night. Now she was dozing off. "Why don't you take over?" she said to Evergreen.

Evergreen was not enthusiastic. But he followed Wild Ginger's wish. "'. . . Those who simply follow the old routine invariably underestimate the people's enthusiasm. Let something new appear and they always disapprove and rush to oppose it' . . . Wild Ginger!" He noticed that Wild Ginger's head was like a hen's pecking grain.

"What's wrong, Evergreen?" Wild Ginger muttered. "Keep going."

"'. . . Afterward, they have to admit defeat and do a little self-criticism. But the next time something new appears, they go through the same process all over again. This is their pattern of behavior in regard to anything and everything new . . .'"

Evergreen slowly put down the Mao book and moved to sit next to Wild Ginger. He paused for a few seconds. When he saw there was no response, he bent his head to reach for her left cheek.

"Go on reading, please." She struggled with her sleepiness and turned her head away.

"'. . . Such people,'" he went on but began to kiss her at the same time, "'. . . are always passive, always fail to move forward at the critical moment . . . and always have to be given a shove in the back before they move a step . . .'" He kissed her neck fervently.

"Pah!" She turned around and slapped him in the face. "We have a contract! Don't tell me that you want to break it!"

He rose. His face was red. "I am quitting."

"Get out, then." Her tone was sharp.

"But . . . you were bored to death and falling asleep yourself."

"How dare you accuse me of being bored with Mao

study! I am not sleepy! You are the problem! Your mind is getting dirtier every day. I am sure you are not here to study Maoism but to enjoy bourgeois indulgence."

He was insulted. In a quick motion he came and grabbed her shoulders. "Why did you insist on making us a team if you are so holy? Why? To keep me here for what? For the pleasure of your eyes? What do you want from me? You know, deep down, you know that we are not interested in Mao but in each other. Our difference is that you won't admit it while I do. I am not ashamed of how I feel. You can't deal with your feelings. I guess being a national icon is more important than being yourself . . . But why drag me along? Why not let me go? Does it give you pleasure to set my feelings on fire and watch me burn?"

"Evergreen, the truth is" — she took a gasp of air — "that I am not burning any less. We have to learn to conquer our weakness. Together we must help each other."

"Wild Ginger, you must not ignore the fact that I don't take being a Maoist as the mission of my life."

"That's not correct, Evergreen. All you need to win is a strong will."

Losing all patience, he shouted, "I despise your will! Your preaching reminds me of those who bound the feet of their girls and castrated their boys!"

"What did I do? What harm have I caused you?" she asked tearfully.

"I can't go on with you." He let her go and turned his face away.

"You've disappointed me." Her tone was cold.

He tried to stay composed but his emotion betrayed him. His facial muscles began to twitch.

She stood up. Her lips moved as if trying to say something. But no sound came out.

He got up, walked toward her.

She stepped back.

He began to open his shirt, button by button.

"What . . . what are you doing?" Her syllables slurred.

He gave no answer but unfastened his belt.

Before she turned away, he stepped out of his pants.

"Animal!" She shut her eyes.

He was erect.

"Traitor! Coward!" she shouted.

He jumped on her and pushed her down under his knees.

She struggled, trying to push him away.

He began to rip off her clothes. Her Mao jacket was pulled open.

Inside the closet, I became short of breath. What should I do? Do I jump out to help?

His hands went to explore her body.

She fought fiercely. But she didn't call my name. I was waiting.

She scratched the skin on his neck.

Finally she got a chance and bit his right shoulder.

He groaned. As if inflamed by the pain he was determined to take her.

They rolled on the floor. They were about eight yards away from me. Wild Ginger was pressed down on her back. He was on top of her. His nose was pointing directly at me.

She screamed.

I cracked open the closet door — my subconscious had taken the scream as a signal to act.

He raised his eyes and suddenly he saw me.

I froze.

We were eye to eye. Evergreen and I.

I couldn't move.

He withdrew.

She sat up, not noticing that Evergreen and I had discovered each other.

He sat himself on the floor like a balloon leaking air.

She buttoned up her clothes and started to fix her hair.

Evergreen got up and put his clothes back on. He went to the water jar and poured himself a bowl of water.

Wild Ginger went to the bathroom behind the wall.

I carefully closed the closet door.

Evergreen sat by the kitchen table. He picked up the Mao book and glanced in my direction.

I stood frozen in place. I wanted to come out, but was afraid that Wild Ginger would be upset. As I pondered what to do next, Wild Ginger reappeared.

"Maybe we can figure out a way to solve this problem," she said. "Chairman Mao teaches us, 'There is no problem that is unsolvable by a true revolutionary.'"

Evergreen put down the Mao book and folded his arms in front of his chest.

"I am here for you, Evergreen, I care about you. It's just . . . I can't have . . . Well, to put it flat and straight . . . I can't commit to a relationship with you. It is not easy for me to be where I am. You must understand that. I have decided to live up to Chairman Mao's expectations."

"You sound like the Ching dynasty empress dowager. You need me to be your eunuch in chief."

"It's unkind of you to say that," she said painfully. "You know that I want to make you happy."

Evergreen laughed bitterly. "By torturing me?"

"I'll do anything for you except make love to you."

Evergreen stood up.

"Wait!" she cried. "I . . . I don't mind if you . . . play with yourself."

It took him a moment to understand what she meant. He sat back down and turned in my direction. As if suddenly reaching a decision, he seemed to relax. Almost happily, he said, "There is one thing you can do to help me."

"I'm listening."

"Read me Mao quotations while I do it."

"You agree with my suggestion then, don't you?" She looked at him. "That we carry on a spiritual relationship?"

"Is that what you want?"

"Yes."

"You don't have to look at me . . ."

"I promise. I will keep my eyes on the lines."

"Are you ready?"

"Sure. Which Mao would you like me to read?"

"Anything."

"How about 'The Struggle in the Chingkang Mountains'? Or 'Introductory Note to How Control of the Wutang Co-operative Shifted from the Middle to the Poor Peasants'?"

"Never mind."

"What's wrong?"

"I feel sick."

When Wild Ginger asked about my time in the closet, I didn't reveal what I'd seen, but I didn't know why. To say that I was afraid to upset Wild Ginger would be untrue. Later as I sorted out my thoughts, I realized that Evergreen's decision to keep his discovery secret from Wild Ginger had been a turning point. In all our time together, I hadn't grown intimately closer to Wild Ginger, but strangely, now I somehow felt closer to Evergreen. It was as if through his silence Evergreen and I were engaged in something together — the betrayal of Wild Ginger.

"You have helped me reach my goal," Wild Ginger said as she made me tea. "It is perfect that Evergreen has come to feel disgusted by his own behavior; he has disabled the power of nature's evil. We've struck a deal. We'll stay close friends and comrades in arms. I'll get to see him every night without risking my future."

"Why do you have to see him every night? Why don't you just leave him alone for good?" I asked almost angrily.

"I wish I knew why, Maple. It's become a craving. I can't bear not to see him every day."

"You are in love. You have been denying the truth."

"Don't apply that bourgeois term to me. I have already told you that such words don't belong in a Maoist's vocabulary. And such sentiments could destroy me. Now swear, Maple, never say that again."

"But you have just said that you couldn't bear not to see him."

"I guess it is the price I have to pay to be a Maoist. Now you know that I'm a piece of real gold — I can stand being hit by a hammer ten thousand times — and still be myself."

"What about him?"

"He just needs to be refined. He is Maoist material. We are a revolutionary pair."

"But the truth is you two fight."

"Well, that's part of the attraction! Did you . . . Maple, did you see him come on me?"

"How could I not see?"

"What did you think?"

"What do you expect me to say?"

"Say what's on your mind."

"It's a jar of porridge there."

"You are good, Maple. You are straight and devil-proof."

"What do you know about me?"

"I know you inside out. I trust you with my most inner secrets. I couldn't be a Maoist without you."

16

The campus smelled of ink and spoiled flour paste. The school seemed another world where wall-to-wall news columns on Mao study discussions were published every other day. Before the first layer of the poster paper dried, the second layer was applied. The traces of dripping ink looked like tears. When the wind blew, the torn papers were swept up in the trees. When it rained, walls of calligraphy were washed away. The lines bled into each other so that the characters were unreadable. The waste was tremendous. No one really read the posters anymore because all of them sounded the same.

We were seventeen years old. We were still studying nothing but Mao. One teacher suggested adding a course of world history, and he was immediately suspected of having an interest in becoming a foreign spy. In geography, we were still on the route that Mao's Red Army traveled during the Long March in 1934. The class dwelt on the same map semester after semester. For tests we had to memorize the names of the villages. We studied no other countries besides Russia, Albania, and North Korea. We didn't know where America was when we shouted "Down with U.S. imperialism!"

"A well-disciplined party armed with the theory of Marxism-Leninism, using the method of self-criticism and linked with the masses of the people . . ." I sat in the classroom bored to death. We had been listening to a broadcast reading of the central party Politburo's latest instruction. ". . . a united front of all revolutionary classes and all revolutionary groups under the leadership of the Communist party — these are the three main weapons with which we have defeated the enemy . . ." I heard the sound but my brain didn't register. The only thing that registered was that the announcers had been changed three times after having exhausted their voices.

Wild Ginger's seat was vacant. She had been absent often since she became the commander in chief of the Red Guard. Owing to lack of sleep, she had grown thin. However, her spirits still seemed high. She spent her day going from school to school promoting Maoism. She lectured around neighborhoods, markets, factories, on public buses, and wherever there were people. She displayed her skill by reciting hundreds of quotations and sang the quotation songs. Her grades in math dropped. It didn't bother her. She believed that if one was a Maoist, one would naturally possess the power to cope with the world. Her best speech continued to be about her meeting with Chairman Mao. Although she had recounted the story hundreds of times, she never grew tired of it and told it vividly. Her emotion affected the audience so much that people were in tears by the end. The crowd rushed to shake hands with her. By touching her, they felt that they had touched Mao.

When night came, Wild Ginger wrestled with her other self. Each evening she returned to the same field to combat her "human weakness." She and Evergreen read hours on end and worked on the papers and speeches. They behaved as if the night of passion never existed. It was hard for me to tell what was on Evergreen's mind. I noticed that something had changed inside me. I couldn't explain why I not only returned to the closet but wanted to stay! I could have walked out for good. All I had to do was to say no to Wild Ginger. But I didn't. I couldn't. I had to be here to find out who I was and what I wanted for myself.

Sunday night Wild Ginger's exhaustion overcame her will — she fell into a dead sleep during the reading. The ink pen she was holding smeared. Struggling to mark the lines in her notebook, her face fell flat onto the page. Evergreen tried to wake her, but it was impossible. He then tried to wipe her nose. Still she wouldn't wake. After holding her head up for a while Evergreen carried her to the bed. Again he tried to shake her. She slept like a dead person. He laid her down and covered her with a blanket. Then he went back and sat on the bench. For the next few minutes he stared at the Mao book.

I became nervous. I sensed something. Before I could think further I heard him say, "Would you come out?"

Involuntarily I uttered a no.

"May I come in?"

I jumped away from the peephole. My duty told me that I ought to say no, ought to go and wake up Wild Ginger, or simply run.

But I didn't do any of these.

I let him walk right into the closet, right into my soul, and change me forever.

17

My arms opened themselves to him as he slipped into the closet, my body receiving him without hesitation. He didn't speak. Neither did I. There was no need. The moment he stepped into the darkness, the world of Mao was behind us. The blossom of the spring fell into my arms as he devoured me. I couldn't get enough of him. His hair smelled of the East China Sea, and I recalled him telling me once that he worked at a seaweed plantation on weekends. He caressed me. My insides cried out in joy. We held each other and I felt him swelling. Time ceased.

I no longer realized where I was.

We lay in silence. Returning to reality was a shock. As he stepped out of the closet I was terrified to think of what would happen next.

There was no movement. Wild Ginger was still sound asleep.

Evergreen left the house while I still lay in the closet. I

heard the door shut. It was two o'clock in the morning. The sound of the clock striking the hour was unusually loud to my ears. I crawled out of the closet. I was concerned that we might have left evidence. But there was none. I felt strange. If my mind couldn't yet grasp what had happened, my body had never felt better.

I left Wild Ginger's house at three o'clock. Walking through the lanes I took a deep breath of fresh air. The night seemed, for the first time, beautiful.

I went home and embraced my pillow. My mind lingered on the strange thought that I was no longer a virgin while Wild Ginger was. I felt bound by guilt yet liberated at the same time. All my frustration had vanished. I wondered what Wild Ginger would do if she could experience this same feeling. Suddenly the idea of devoting one's entire life to Mao was not only dull but ridiculous.

I had a dream in which Wild Ginger visited me. "I was collecting candy wrappers in the streets," she told me. "I came home with my handbag filled with dirty wrappers. I soaked them and washed them carefully with soapy water. I pasted them one by one onto the tiles in the bathroom. The whole wall was covered. The beauty was extraordinary. I sat and looked at it for hours on end. The flowers, leaves, animals, and rocks. A wall of spring. When the wrappers dried, I peeled them off and inserted them between the pages of my books. They saved me from the boredom of the Mao studies."

·   ·   ·

I wasn't eager to go to school, because I was afraid of seeing Wild Ginger. The whole morning I lay in bed and pretended to be sick. Then Wild Ginger came. It was afternoon. She seemed to be in good spirits and was in her regular army uniform. She brought my mother a string of garlic and strode directly to my bed.

I sat up, like a criminal being confronted by a policeman.

"Are you all right?" She looked concerned and reached out her hand to feel my forehead. "No fever. What's wrong?"

I realized that she didn't know what had happened last night. I pushed her hand away. "I am just a little tired."

"Is it because I made you stay in the closet for too long?"

"Of course not." I hopped out of the bed. "That wasn't a problem. Not at all."

"I am sorry I fell asleep last night. Evergreen left. He just left and hasn't come back. I am sure he's upset. But he doesn't have to worry about it, I'll make it up to him. He loves to be with me. I could be reading anything and he wouldn't care." She smiled.

I found myself suddenly annoyed by her smile. I remained silent and began to put on my shoes.

"What did you do after he left?"

"Me?" I kicked off my shoes and then put them back on again. "What do you mean? Would you . . . like to have a cup of water?"

"No thanks. I suppose you didn't take off with him, did you?"

146

"No, of course not. You told me that you didn't want him to know that I was there, didn't you?"

"No."

"Is it cold outside?" I tried to hide my nervousness.

"What did you do, then?" She raised her chin and looked into my eyes.

"I . . ."

She began to laugh. "It's all right to tell the truth."

"Truth? What truth?"

"I mean, it's all right to say that you fell asleep too and that you did nothing else."

"I did fall asleep. Of course."

What had happened seemed unreal to me. It had been a week and the three of us had lost contact. It was as if we were waiting for something. I wasn't clear about my feelings. I couldn't stop replaying what had taken place in the closet. I began to feel that I could never be the same way with Wild Ginger. I wouldn't admit that I had betrayed her. Yet I couldn't say that I didn't betray her. I had enjoyed Evergreen shamelessly. I felt lucky for what had happened. Evergreen and I had offered each other something we craved — human affection. I was too desperate and too selfish to reject him. I had always envied Evergreen and Wild Ginger. I had always wanted to be in Wild Ginger's place. It was long before Evergreen came to me. I encouraged him by not reporting to Wild Ginger the moment he and I discovered each other. My excuse was that she never wanted Evergreen physically. If they had been lovers, I would never have allowed myself to interfere.

On the tenth day, I received a letter from Evergreen. He asked if I could meet him that evening in his friend's apartment on Big Dipper Road. My excitement was beyond belief. I went at the appointed time, eight-thirty, to the apartment building, which faced the street. The place was on the second floor over a basket shop. The staircase was filthy and dusty. It was crowded with baskets. The wooden stairs squeaked under my feet. I stood in front of a narrow door. I knocked. A skinny middle-aged man opened the door. He let me in without a word and he left as I entered. I heard him locking the door.

"Hello." Evergreen's voice greeted me in the dark.

"I need to see."

"I'm lighting a candle."

"Is it safe?"

"Mr. Xing is the bellman of the neighborhood. Nobody bothers him." The candle was dim like a ghost's eye.

"How did you bribe him?"

"He needs food coupons. His family is dying of hunger in the countryside."

I took a deep breath as he began to kiss me.

"No guilt?" he asked. "I was afraid that you might regret what happened."

I told him that I wasn't thinking. I couldn't. I was out and beyond myself.

"Same here," he said, blowing out the candle.

The room was now completely dark.

Downstairs came the noise of basket makers. They were talking in a strange dialect, yelling and laughing at the same time.

Evergreen came to me in silence. It felt as if we had been lovers for years — our bodies knew exactly how to please each other.

"Let's be the reactionaries, let's burn down the house of Mao," he whispered.

We repeated the pleasure again and again.

Downstairs grew quiet. The midnight shift workers had gone. I was beginning to feel tired. But Evergreen wouldn't quit.

He sat next to me by the candle and watched me eat the snack he'd brought.

"Why don't you have more buns?" I asked.

"Sure." He leaned over and said, "Take off your shirt."

"No. Why?"

"I hunger only for you."

I began to laugh. "Go chew Mao quotations! Fill your stomach with them. Come on! Chairman Mao teaches us . . ."

"'A thousand years is too long, seize the moment.'" He grabbed me. "Chairman Mao also teaches us, 'A revolution is an insurrection, an act of violence by which one class overthrows another.'"

"Chairman Mao again teaches us" — I put down the buns and wrestled with him — "'The situation must change. It is the task of the people of the whole world to put an end to the aggression and oppression perpetrated by imperialism.'"

He went wild. "'If the U.S. monopoly capitalist groups persist in pushing their policies of aggression and war, the day is bound to come when they will be hanged by the people of the whole world.'"

I could feel my body blooming. I was unable to continue the reciting.

"Don't you stop, Maple! Show your faith in Chairman Mao! Demonstrate your loyalty! Page one hundred fifty-six. 'Speech at the Moscow Meeting of Communist and Workers' Parties.' Come on, now!"

"'It is my opinion,'" I began, "'that the international situation has now reached a new turning point.'" I stopped, my thoughts suddenly scattered — the pleasure was too overwhelming.

"Go on, Maple, go on. 'There are two winds in the world today'" — he caressed me, his hands cupping my breasts from behind — "'the East Wind and the West Wind. There is a Chinese saying, *Either the East Wind prevails over the West Wind or the West Wind prevails over the East Wind.*'"

We were breathless. He insisted we continue reciting. I tasted his sweat as I went on. "'It is characteristic of the situation today that the East Wind is prevailing over the West Wind. That is to say, the forces of socialism have become overwhelmingly superior to the forces of imperialism . . .'"

Our bodies came together again.

The mind's scene was splendid.

"Say yes, Maple, say yes! Say you want me too, say it! I need to hear you say it!"

My tears streamed.

"Yes! Do that again, Maple, yes!"

"Chairman Mao teaches us . . ."

"No."

"Come on, Evergreen!"

"'People . . . people of the world, unite and defeat the U.S. aggressors and all their running dogs! People of the world, be courageous, dare to fight, defy difficulties, and advance wave upon waves.'"

"'Then the whole world will belong to the people. Monsters of all kinds shall be destroyed!'"

"'Keep pushing the cart,' Maple!"

"'Keep pushing the cart until . . . until we reach the Communist heaven!'"

"Oh Maple, the blind man is picking peaches."

"And the blind woman has caught a fat fish — this is a miracle."

"Do the quotations!"

"You armchair revolutionary!"

He groaned, "Oh! Chairman Mao!"

The night didn't end until we collapsed in each other's arms. I meant to talk about what to do with Wild Ginger but didn't get a chance. To be honest, I was avoiding the discussion. The problem had grown too big to be fixed. In the meantime Evergreen and I were testing each other. Before I could do anything regarding Wild Ginger I needed to know my feelings as well as Evergreen's. Nevertheless I feared that I had no control of the situation. Wild Ginger could break in any moment. I had, in fact, been waiting for it to happen. She always had a foreboding before her fate took shape. I could smell the scorched words in her mouth.

I continued to avoid Wild Ginger. Luckily all her time was being taken up with a big campaign to promote Mao's latest teachings. There was an accident — an "accident" in Wild Ginger's eyes, but not in mine. It chilled my enthusiasm completely for the Maoists. A high school student, a piano player, had criticized the Red Guards for destroying his piano. A fight broke out and the Red Guards placed the pianist's hand in a doorjamb and slammed the door shut.

Wild Ginger rushed to the spot. "The man could have played Mao quotation songs! I know him. His name is Guo-Dong the Grand Beam. He is a good comrade. We had talked about having him play the solo for the Shanghai Mao Propaganda Band. He was my responsibility! And now you have ruined my plan!" She ordered the door slammer to be immediately arrested and sentenced to life in prison.

To all of us the sentence was too harsh. Wild Ginger had been acting strangely recently. Her voice was distant and her expression remote. Her eyes looked weary although still penetrating. Something seemed to be seriously bothering her and she was constantly angry.

I ran toward home as if someone were chasing me. It was my own thoughts. Evergreen and I hadn't met for a month. Had he gone back to Wild Ginger? Or had she caught him and made him confess? I had a feeling that the confrontation between me and Wild Ginger was about to take place.

The neighborhood was quiet that noon. The midsummer heat was stifling. Fat locusts infested the trees and made high-pitched noises. I slowed as I neared the lane. I noticed a shadow under the sun. It was Evergreen.

"Wild Ginger and I are finished," he began.

I felt bad and relieved at the same time.

"Last night I made up my mind. I went to her house." Evergreen's voice was strained. "She . . . actually knew. The moment I mentioned your name she came and slapped me in the face. She told me that she didn't want to know the details. She didn't cry or anything. She . . . led me to her bed."

My hair began to prickle at its roots.

"She stripped herself and said that she would give me what I wanted. Even if it meant that she would have to lie to keep her position."

I squatted down by the roots of a tree and waited for him to continue.

"I could hardly think at that moment." He knelt down next to me and lowered his voice as much as he could. "I . . .

tried to hold on to my clothes when she tried to strip me. She was . . . I don't know how to describe it. I couldn't tell if she was herself. Anyway, she wouldn't let me go . . . She insisted on us going to bed. I told her that I couldn't do it. I . . . I didn't want to hurt her feelings, so I said that it was not worth it. She should have her first time with someone who would appreciate it. Then she cried."

My tears welled up.

"She said that she had put her shame in my hands and that I was . . . obligated to pity her and show mercy if I had a conscience. . . It was . . . awful. She slapped her own face when I refused to touch her. She began to hit her head against the wall, said that she was sorry to Chairman Mao, said that she was going to whip the beast out of her body. The sound of her banging her head on the wall devastated me. I begged her to stop and . . . I said I would try to take her.

"It felt like making love to the dead. She was underneath me, her eyes were shut, her legs apart, her jaws locked tightly, as if she were going through torture . . . But she wouldn't let me go. She cried, 'You must finish me!' In the meantime she wouldn't stop talking and reciting Mao quotations. She yelled at me, 'Prove that you are not a coward, admit that you are evil seduced. Show your shame, take out your sun instrument and look at it, spit on it . . .' Oh, these terrible words! I can't get them out of my ears! I thought I was mad to hear that. I am sorry, Maple, I shouldn't put you through this . . .'"

"Go on, please. I need to know."

"She said it was her turn. She must toss herself in the pit of shame. She must see for herself how grotesque coupling was. She pulled over a mirror and demanded that I look at myself while taking her. The ugly members of our bodies. She said, 'Don't you think they are the most disgusting organs? One is like a worm and the other like a bee's nest! One should be cut and the other scorched!' She made me hate my body. I really did at that moment. I could have thrown up. She said it was the right feeling. The disgust. Keep looking. I can still see her shouting in front of my eyes. 'What are these? Animals! Animals!'

"I was completely impotent . . . I begged her to quit, but she said that we must fix the problem. It was only sex that blocked my eyes to see my own potential as a great Maoist. She said I could be fixed if I let her help. She said, 'You must get erect. I must go through this in order to get it out of your system. We must do this so there will be no myth between our bodies.' I tried to explain but she refused to listen. She pushed herself onto me, all over, and my body started to betray me and then . . . suddenly" — Evergreen paused to catch his breath, his shoulders trembled, and his face turned paper white — "I saw blood."

18

I couldn't sleep. I felt that I owed Wild Ginger an explanation. I had become clear about my feelings toward Evergreen. After our talk Evergreen wrote me a letter. "To me, Maple, love is more important than Maoism."

After contemplation, I wrote back. I accepted his proposal of engagement, however with one condition: I would not further my relationship with him before I made peace with Wild Ginger. Wild Ginger was too important to my life. And I was determined to keep her friendship.

It was two o'clock in the morning. My mind had been racing. Finally I got up and sneaked out of the house. I wandered around the streets and then found myself at Wild Ginger's door. Her light was on. I stood, trying to figure out whether or not to knock. Suddenly the door opened. Wild Ginger in her uniform stood in front of me.

"I don't intend to spit on you but I might not be able to help myself," she said. "Go away, Maple."

"Wild Ginger," I uttered weakly. "I need a chance."

"Go away before I pick up a gun and shoot you in the head."

"Please, Wild Ginger, I'll do what you ask, anything."

She laughed. "Anything? Who are you fooling? Don't say it if you don't mean it!"

"I mean it."

"What about giving up Evergreen? Now tell me that you mean it!"

I lowered my head.

"How blind I was to trust you . . . How I hate myself!"

"Please, Wild Ginger, I am . . ." It was as if my mouth were not mine. I tried to drag more words out of it but my thoughts scattered. I watched Wild Ginger talk but I couldn't hear her. I saw her mouthing "I hate myself." Suddenly my mind was stirred by the image of years ago in which she stabbed her hand with a sharpened pencil.

I began to feel that I could never truly love Evergreen, that the relationship between Evergreen and me would never work because it would always be haunted. It was doomed right from the beginning — I loved Wild Ginger so much that her suffering over Evergreen was my curse.

She pushed me out and slammed the door.

I stood there, unable to think.

I can't remember how long I stood. Dawn broke. The locusts had begun their chorus. The noise was piercing and getting louder by the moment. The sound filled my head.

For the next three months Wild Ginger and I didn't talk. The pain not only didn't go away but deepened. We were almost eighteen. Bored with Mao study I retreated into my own world where missing-cover Western novels and hand-copied ancient manuscripts became my obsession. Evergreen resigned his post as the district Red Guard head. He was in a military training program preparing to go to Vietnam. We couldn't make ourselves stay away from each other.

Wild Ginger turned into an unrecognizable character. She set laws for all the youth — anyone who was caught engaging in a sexual act would be considered a criminal. She personally took charge of several raids where the Red Guards broke into people's houses.

I sensed that Wild Ginger was looking to catch us.

It was as if I weren't walking on my own legs that morning. I ate no breakfast. After I came back from the market I headed for school. As I approached the classroom, I saw Hot Pepper chatting intimately with Wild Ginger. Hot Pepper was dressed in a blouse printed in a pattern of pine trees and falling snow. Wild Ginger was in a navy blue Mao jacket with a bright red collar. She was examining an application of some sort, which I was sure Hot Pepper had completed. As I got closer and saw the red letterhead I was able to tell that it was Hot Pepper's application for Communist party membership.

Seeing me, Wild Ginger put her arm around Hot Pepper's shoulders and the two turned and walked away. Within two weeks Hot Pepper was pronounced a party member. She followed Wild Ginger like a dog. She carried a heavy paste bucket all day long to help Wild Ginger put up news columns. I saw her pour Wild Ginger water during her speeches. The two flattered each other at the Mao activists' conventions. Hot Pepper must have felt an inch taller when she ran into me in the neighborhood. She gave me a warning for being late for last Thursday's Mao quotation reciting.

As a radical Maoist, Wild Ginger not only pushed herself, but also pushed the entire district to be the model of Mao studies. In the name of Mao she enslaved us. We worked on reciting the quotations like monks chanting Buddhist scriptures. There was no longer time even for me to go to the market. Every morning Wild Ginger's shrill whistle would come from the loudspeakers mounted on the electric poles throughout the neighborhood. I often rushed to the school without washing my face or brushing my teeth. Within minutes the entire school would gather in an open square.

Wild Ginger would stand on a four-foot-high concrete stage. The microphone in her hand looked like a grenade. Her skin was sunburned. Her eyes blinked nervously and her hands made fists. She often started out with a controlled voice but then, in an instant, she would shout. The sound would blast and the microphone would buzz. After a brief Mao quotation reciting, she would order us to march and run. She would keep us going so long we sometimes wondered if she had forgotten about us. Anyone who dropped out would be publicly humiliated and punished.

When we ran into each other she treated me like a wall. One time she laughed hysterically when our shoulders brushed. I saw her showing more affection toward Hot Pepper. If Hot Pepper had a tail she would have wagged it harder. I knew she had been coveting a chair at the Red Guard's headquarters.

19

When my mother asked me about Wild Ginger I lied. I figured that she had some idea about our breaking up. She seemed just as awkward around the subject as I was.

At the end of summer, Evergreen returned from military training. At the train station where I went to pick him up we discussed our future. "I have changed my mind about wanting to go to Vietnam," he began. "I'd like to open a husband-and-wife elementary school for poor children in a remote village in the countryside." After a pause he asked, "Would you like to be the wife?"

Without thinking, I answered yes. I wanted to escape as much as he did since I had failed to make peace with Wild Ginger. "You would have to wait until I graduate from the middle school," I added. He was thrilled. The idea of being with Evergreen, away from Wild Ginger, and teaching children was both appealing and exciting. The options for graduates were not encouraging in 1973. Shanghai's population had exploded and the city was terribly overcrowded. There was little demand for workers. One's best option, if one qualified, was to become a city sanitation worker. The rest would be sent to labor collectives in the remote countryside. A person's fate depended on family background, the level of his or her loyalty toward Mao, and the government's quota the family owed.

When I broke the news to my parents, they were quiet. They weren't sure if it was a good idea for me to become engaged at eighteen. I explained that our love was strong. Finally my parents granted me silent permission. When Evergreen started to receive "congratulation" candies from the neighbors he cautioned me to "be careful of Wild Ginger." I couldn't think of Wild Ginger as dangerous, so didn't take his words too seriously.

"She might not mean to harm you," Evergreen warned, "but she is insane."

"Well, she needs time to heal, and after all we are the cause of her pain."

"I don't think that we should blame ourselves for her misery," Evergreen disagreed. "She had made it clear at the very beginning, to both of us, that being a Maoist was more important to her than being human. I was not what she wanted. To make a bad joke — you picked up her leftovers."

I didn't want to argue with Evergreen. I believed that Wild Ginger loved Evergreen. It was a part of herself that she couldn't understand, didn't know what to do with. I had taken advantage of her confusion. I was the thief. I was prepared to face Wild Ginger's rage one day. I needed that combat; I needed her to slap me in the face. It would be a kindness, forgiveness, and blessing.

20

"We're organizing a Mao quotation-singing rally!" Wild Ginger's voice came through a loudspeaker. "The Cultural Revolution is in its seventh year, and the struggle between the proletarian class and the bourgeois class has intensified ever more significantly. Defending Maoism and demonstrating the proletarian class's strength is not only important but absolutely necessary. We must sing loud, louder, and louder the Mao quotation songs. We must promote hard, harder, and hardest the ideas of Maoism! The rally will be held in the Shanghai Acrobatics Stadium!"

The city was mobilized. Hot Pepper led a thousand-member team and distributed leaflets at every street corner. People were ordered to put down whatever they were doing to join the event. The factories, labor collectives, and schools were required by the city committee to send a delegation of singers to the rally.

As the executive producer, Wild Ginger selected the delegations and scheduled their auditions. She discussed her ideas with the orchestra, stage designers, and technicians on sound, lights, and props. She conducted the practices, rehearsals, and run-throughs. On the surface her energy seemed inexhaustible, but I could tell beneath her smiling face she was falling apart. There was a detectable nervousness in her voice. People who worked with her talked about her unpredictable outbursts and mood swings. The way she shouted and yelled for no particular reason. Her habit of smashing things. Her use of profanity.

Although Evergreen and I had no interest in joining the rally, our names were called and we had no choice but to go to the Acrobatics Stadium for practice.

The practice was a three-week, daylong commitment involving fifteen thousand people from over five hundred work units. Each group was called to stand up and sing until Wild Ginger gave her approval. Some groups were good. The Shanghai Garrison was disciplined, with a tradition of singing, and had obviously been practicing. But the peasant groups were lousy. They were sent by the commune and had hardly sung in their lives. They sang off-key and confused Mao quotation songs with their folk songs. Wild Ginger did as much as she could to help them but finally she had to give up. "As long as you show me that you can follow the beat, I will pass you," she told them. The school groups were the best, but the young children had little patience. When it wasn't their turn, they sneaked around the bowl-shaped stadium and looked for their friends and neighbors to play.

Evergreen's group was about two gates away from me. I saw him sitting quietly, reading *The Electrician's Guide*. I didn't understand why Wild Ginger insisted on having us. It was awkward to meet like strangers.

Evergreen and I fought over whether or not to continue attending Wild Ginger's rehearsals. Encounters with her had become unbearable for him. I didn't want to go either, but I was concerned that we would be singled out in ways that would jeopardize our future. Evergreen disagreed.

We were in a vegetable patch somewhere in the suburbs. It was night. We were afraid of Wild Ginger's spies so we traveled as far as the public bus would take us. But still, we couldn't escape Wild Ginger. Whenever we opened our mouths, her name popped out. Even in the middle of passion my mind would slip and I would feel a wave of guilt wash over me. Evergreen was affected, but he couldn't loosen Wild Ginger's hold on my mind. Soon he was frustrated. "We'll leave Shanghai as soon as we can."

I was unsure about Evergreen's feelings about Wild Ginger. He wanted so badly to get away from her. But my conscience kept telling me that it was because he wanted her. Maybe we both wanted Wild Ginger so much that we couldn't stand it.

To avoid mentioning Wild Ginger we ceased talking. We

would meet at the station, get on the bus, and sit silently until our destination. When we got off the bus I would follow him. We would walk miles until he located a quiet spot. Our usual place was in a cow shed behind fields of yecai. We would climb over the packed hay to hide ourselves. He would lay his raincoat down and I would offer him my body. It had become a ritual, a way to get the frustration out of ourselves.

I had trouble looking at him because Wild Ginger was so much on my mind. I kept seeing her eyes. Yet I dared not speak about my thoughts. I would get on my knees and look at the cows. I asked Evergreen to do whatever he liked with my body while I thought about my future with him, a future without Wild Ginger. And then I would be aroused.

I could feel his tension — his pleasure often came in the middle of our shared pain. Too many times I saw tears in his eyes. He wouldn't speak about his thoughts either. I knew he was thinking of her too. I told him that it was all right. Everything would be all right. It would be over soon and we would survive. At that moment he broke down and he was free. I received and calmed him until he became full of desire again.

One night things became unbearable for me. I asked him to call me by her name. Before he could react I started to talk like Wild Ginger. I started to recite Mao quotations the way Wild Ginger would. I copied her tone and style. I recited the quotations as I unzipped his trousers.

He took me as I continued to recite. It was Wild Ginger's

favorite paragraph: "Volume three, page thirty, 'Rectify the Party's Style of Work.' 'So long as a person who has made mistakes does not hide his sickness for fear of treatment or persist in his mistakes until he is beyond cure, so long as he honestly and sincerely wishes to be cured and to mend his ways, we should welcome him and cure his sickness so that he can become a good comrade.'" I rode him as he moved gently inside me. Through the sound of his breath I stared out into the night. I envisioned Wild Ginger. She stood in uniform with her front buttons open. Her breasts were two steaming buns.

I took Evergreen's hands. I asked him to close his eyes. I asked him to touch me, to feel me, feel Wild Ginger. "'We can never succeed if we just let ourselves go and lash out at the comrade with shortcomings. In treating an ideological or a political malady, one must never be rough and rash but must adopt the approach of curing the sickness to save the patient, which is the only correct and effective method.'"

And then I closed my own eyes and once again I was in Wild Ginger's closet.

21

Finally the rally came. The afternoon was cold and windy. The temperature continued to drop. A big crowd milled in front of the stadium. The singing groups started to arrive. My group head, a guy nicknamed "Shorty," was upset with me. "Don't take it so lightly! It is a political assignment. It is much more important than finishing your lunch." He asked if I was wearing a white shirt underneath and whether I had brought the straw hat that he had requested. I reported that I had the white shirt but had forgotten the hat. "Go home and get it!" he yelled. "You know, our group has been appointed to play peasants. Wild Ginger will shower my face with spit if I have my members wear the wrong costumes. Her reputation is on the line. She's giving us our chance to show loyalty toward Chairman Mao. It is an honorable assignment! And there is no room for mistakes. Please sing as loudly as you can. Sing at the top of your lungs!"

After I fetched my hat my group entered the stadium. It was dim and smelled filthy. Sitting on benches that circled from bottom to top, thousands of people were preparing themselves. The noise was deafening. I stood on the west side at row thirty-seven. As I looked around for Evergreen, Shorty came with props. They were sunflowers made of cardboard. He asked me to help distribute them. "Sway the flowers from side to side when singing. Now let's practice 'Talks at the Yenan Forum on Literature and Art.' Ready? Begin. 'Our great savior, great leader, great helmsman, and great commander Chairman Mao teaches us . . .'"

As our group practiced the drill, other groups joined in. All of a sudden, the air boiled. I swayed my props and sang, "'In the world today all culture, all literature and art belong to definite classes and are geared to definite political lines.'" I looked for Evergreen and located him way up in the back by an exit door. "'There is in fact no such thing as art for art's sake, art that stands above classes, art that is detached from or independent of politics.'" He was not reading *The Electrician's Guide* this time. But he looked terribly bored. He had been attending electricians' workshops and classes. His mind had already gone to the remote village. He told me that we had to prepare for a place where no one had ever seen a lightbulb. He had a dream of putting lights in village kitchens and motors in farming machines. I encouraged him. I had been spending my savings to buy him pliers and wires.

Evergreen saw me. He waved his sunflower. I waved back and sang, "'Proletarian literature and art are part of the whole proletarian revolutionary cause; they are, as Lenin said, cogs and wheels in the whole revolutionary machine.'" He smiled and cautioned me with his eyes not to stare at him. I thought about the dinner my parents had invited him to several days ago. It was a way for them to acknowledge him as their future son-in-law. The day before, he had offered to install a shower bath for my family. My mother was pleased. It was her dream to have a shower. Evergreen came in the morning with three of his friends. The men didn't stop working until late night. They put up a giant wooden bucket in the corner of our kitchen with plastic draperies. When it was time to demonstrate the shower, not only did the showerhead not work, the fuses blew. Evergreen was embarrassed. It turned out that in his nervousness he had misconnected the wires. My parents were impressed by his effort. The shower finally worked and my parents started to help me pack for my life's journey with Evergreen.

At the bottom of the stands, Wild Ginger stood with the Shanghai Orchestra at her back. The conductor wore white gloves. His fingers spiked out like chopsticks. I recognized him. He was the young pianist whose hand had been destroyed by the Red Guards.

Wild Ginger directed the swarming crowds into their places. The microphone in her hand kept malfunctioning. One minute it buzzed, the next it was fine. A few minutes later it was dead again.

Hot Pepper ran around Wild Ginger's feet trying to reconnect the wires. She tapped the microphone to test the sound and then ran up and down the staircases to check the volume. I had no idea how Wild Ginger and Hot Pepper could possibly get along. I knew how little Wild Ginger used to think of Hot Pepper. She used to say that Hot Pepper would never need a cardiologist because she had no heart. Did she think Hot Pepper had a heart now? When Hot Pepper was accepted as a Communist party member she said, "I was a piece of shit before Wild Ginger took me in." I wondered if Wild Ginger found the relationship fulfilling.

The lights brightened. The crowd cheered. Wild Ginger announced the opening of the rally. We sang the national anthem, "The Red in the East." The "workers" challenged the "peasants." Then the "peasants" challenged the "soldiers" and the "students."

"Wasn't that an awfully good song?" Wild Ginger shouted.

"Yes!" the crowd responded.

"Another one, yes?"

"Yes!"

The shouts were followed by thunderous applause.

The way our group sang depended on Shorty's gymnastics. When his arms swayed like a willow in a storm, we pitched. When the arms moved like a sweeping broom, we wailed. The paper petals of my sunflowers began to drop. The men and women next to me screamed as loudly as they could. It made Shorty happy.

The sound rose and fell in waves. After the "soldiers" sang "The People's Army Loves People," we came to our last song, "On Youth." My throat hurt badly.

"'The world is yours, as well as ours, but in the last analysis, it is yours. You are the young people. You are full of vigor and vitality. You are in the bloom of life . . .'" In the midst of the song I noticed a few foreigners in front of the stage with cameras in their hands. They were accompanied by a gray-haired man. The foreigners smiled as they flashed their cameras.

"It's the new general party secretary of Shanghai!" someone said.

"'. . . like the sun at eight or nine in the morning,'" I shouted, "'China's hope is placed on you . . .'"

Many years later when I recalled this scene, I asked myself why Wild Ginger hadn't introduce the gray-haired man and his guests to the rally. If she had, I might have figured out why she was so nervous. She was like the driver of a speeding train who suddenly realized that the track had been wrongly connected and that he was about to smash into a train speeding from the opposite direction. And there was no way she could stop the train.

"'. . . The world belongs to you. China's future belongs to you!'" I remember squeezing my gut to reach the high note.

Suddenly the lights went off. The stadium was a black hole. After a moment of shocking silence, we heard Wild Ginger's voice, shaky and disoriented. "Calm . . . down, calm down, comrades, there is an . . . an . . . Anyway, we have sent someone to fix . . . This is not a problem. I appreciate the loyalty toward Chairman Mao you all display. I am proud . . . And you should be proud of yourself. Everything is fine, comrades. Listen to me. The lights will be on in a second." Her microphone buzzed and we could no longer hear her.

There were whistles in the dark. The crowd began to talk among themselves. Someone started to throw the props.

A moment later Wild Ginger's voice rose. "Comrades! The darkness has shut our eyes, but it can't shut our voices, can it?"

"No!"

"Let's sing 'The world belongs to you and China's future belongs to you' one more time. Ready? Begin!"

We sang. I had no idea that my future had just been forever altered.

When the lights came back on I saw a group of security guards rush in. They escorted the general party secretary and his foreign guests out of the stadium. The secretary looked terribly upset. He kept pointing his finger at Wild Ginger. Wild Ginger tried to explain but he walked out.

Wild Ginger was abandoned right in front of the entire stadium. She stood with her microphone dangling at her side and her mouth half open, like a melting snowman under the sun.

The guards came back. They were led by Hot Pepper. The crowd watched them as they moved toward the top of the bleachers. They stopped at the last bench where Evergreen sat with his group.

My mind had a hard time interpreting what my eyes were seeing. I started to gasp in disbelief: Hot Pepper pointed at Evergreen and the guards went up and handcuffed him.

Before Evergreen could struggle the men took him away.

Hot Pepper grabbed Evergreen's bag from underneath the bench. The bag seemed extremely heavy in her hand. I was sure it was filled with books and tools. When Hot Pepper reached Wild Ginger she held the bag high. Grabbing the microphone from Wild Ginger, Hot Pepper made an announcement to the crowd. Her mice eyes were lit with excitement. "Here is the anti-Maoist who is responsible for tonight's incident!" Hot Pepper took out Evergreen's pliers and wrench from the bag. "The tools for the crime are in this bag. He ruined the rally by sabotaging the power!"

The crowd was stunned.

Wild Ginger grabbed the microphone back from Hot Pepper and covered it with her hand. The two argued.

"Why can't we talk here?" Hot Pepper yelled as she turned toward the crowd. "Didn't Chairman Mao teach us, 'A true Communist has nothing to hide from her people'?"

Wild Ginger backed off. She moved like an old lady. Her posture slumped, and her legs began to shake.

22

I was not aware of what I was doing when I plunged through the crowd and headed toward the back of the stage. I was driven by one thought, to speak with Wild Ginger. I was sure she was behind the incident. Surely she must be. And yet her reaction on the stage confused me.

When I passed one of the prop rooms I heard an angry conversation behind the panels. My ear immediately registered the voices — Wild Ginger's and Hot Pepper's. Quickly I hid myself.

"Well, no use arguing now. The job is done." It was Hot Pepper's voice. It was filled with elation.

"Why did you invite the general party secretary without my permission?" Wild Ginger's voice was strained with anger.

"Don't you want to pull a weed by its root? You wanted to stain Evergreen in order to separate the couple and I helped you and did it thoroughly."

"You bitch! I specifically instructed you not to send an invitation to the secretary, didn't I?"

"Yes you did. I understood your intention perfectly. You didn't want to turn this into a political incident. You wanted to maintain control. You wanted to have him singed but not killed. You have feelings for him. You wanted to send your friend Maple into exile while you got your man back. What a wonderful plot! A reactionary discovered and you get to be the judge. Oh, you must really believe that you are powerful. But who is the fool here?"

"Hot Pepper!"

"Yes, Commander. I only spared a little creativity when carrying out your order. I invited the general party secretary and his foreign guests. I made it a political incident. I succeeded in ruining you! That's right, I have ruined you."

"You snake! For heaven's sake, I sponsored you to become a party member! How can you be so ungrateful?"

"Ungrateful? You must really think that I have forgotten how you took away my popularity at the school. I hate you so much I could drink poison. It is I who should have been the one to meet Chairman Mao; it is I who should have been called the heroine. You ripped away my opportunity and happiness . . ." Hot Pepper broke into tears. "Oh, Chairman Mao, today is my day, finally. Let me recite your teaching: 'If I am not attacked, I won't launch an attack. And if I am attacked, you can be sure that I will counterattack.'"

"I should have murdered you."

"Precisely. Now there is nothing you can do to reverse

the situation. The incident was caught by the foreign cameras. It has now become a national embarrassment. The general party secretary's shame. Evergreen has committed a crime that insulted Chairman Mao! I am thrilled. And the best part is that you can't afford to expose the truth. Because if you do, you'll destroy yourself. You have to keep bribing me to be silent."

"If I had the power to create this mess, I have the power to fix it."

"Of course you could turn yourself in. Won't that be my dream come true! Once you told me that I was too stupid to do basic logic and math, remember? Now allow me to show you the progress I have made: this is a recent example of the law of this country. On May twenty-second, 1972, a thief stole a citizen's purse. He was sentenced to one year in jail. In the same month, a different date, another thief who stole a foreigner's purse was given a death sentence. Reason? He brought shame to the nation. Chairman Mao has been trying to show the world that China is crimeless — his teaching has reformed a society into a great moral model of mankind. You see, I have been blessed."

Silence. I could hear Wild Ginger clench her teeth. "I will get Evergreen off the hook. Just watch me."

Hot Pepper struck a match and lit a cigarette. The smoke drifted over. "Remember how you took my umbrella away from me years ago? It's my turn to kick the dog."

· · ·

I was caught by a strange force the moment Hot Pepper mentioned the word "umbrella." The image of Wild Ginger rescuing me from Hot Pepper's beating was before my eyes. Suddenly enraged, I rushed forward.

Both Wild Ginger and Hot Pepper heard the noise and turned around.

"Aha, Maple, are you here to congratulate me in my victory or share in the misery of Wild Ginger's defeat?" Hot Pepper took a long drag from her cigarette and smiled viciously. "Allow me to sign off, Commander."

Silently Wild Ginger and I stared at each other.

"What do you want?" Her voice was filled with ice.

"May I speak to you?"

"No." She turned around and marched out.

23

There was no way to obtain statistics, but 1973 was a year of severe sentences and countless executions. The nation reeled from forces within and without owing to the nation's instability. Internationally, the Vietnamese Communists battled the Americans just to the south. There were riots in Russia and food shortages in North Korea. The domestic picture was bleak too. Mao's disciple, his most trusted comrade in arms and his chosen successor, Vice Chairman Lin Biao, was suddenly pronounced an assassin and a Russian spy. Every week new execution lists were posted around the neighborhood. In Chia Chia Lane alone, two young people were executed and eleven more arrested. The criminals' faces were printed on the bulletins and their names were split so that the word "convict" could be inserted. Their faces were photographed in the moment of shock. The expressions were distorted, with lips drawn back over stained, crooked teeth. Mothers would not let their children go near the posters. Nobody told us that the party was under tremendous pressure because the Cultural Revolution had led to the collapse of the country's economy. Mao worship dissipated and the nation began to lose faith in Communism.

The central Politburo's nervousness began to spread. The local authorities were instructed to apply "heavy drugs" to combat the "anti-Mao virus." Wild Ginger was caught in the spinning of this whirlpool. Not only did she fail to get Evergreen off the hook, she herself was questioned by the general party secretary. Evergreen's case was taken out of her control and transferred to the people's municipal court. The court declared Evergreen an anti-Maoist and ordered him put to death.

My conscience told me to expose Wild Ginger the moment I learned the news. It was the only way to save Evergreen. But when I pictured Wild Ginger's execution, my determination crumbled. I couldn't escape the image of her sweeping the lane at four o'clock in the morning. Again and again in my dreams I felt her tears running down my cheeks and heard her cry, "Maple, my mother hanged herself!"

Would I be able to live with my decision and the torture that came with it if I turned her in?

"I'm not going to wash my hand from now on." I woke up in the middle of the night remembering what she had said to me the day she got back from meeting Chairman Mao. She was in rapture.

"I shook hands with Chairman Mao. It was the happiest

moment in my life! This is the hand. Touch it, Maple. My right hand. This is what the great savior touched. Look at this, feel it, the warmth, Maple, doesn't your heart feel the power? Shake it, shake it again. I have shared this great warmth with over a thousand people just today. I have been shaking hands from morning to evening. One old lady fainted in joy after she barely touched my fingers. She said she felt the current. She said it was the Buddha's power."

I looked at Wild Ginger's glowing face. Was she talking to me? Those red cheeks, those happy almond eyes. The sweetness of her mood touched me. Within the yellow bursts of her pupils I saw Mao waving his hand.

She had then told me of the picture she had taken with Chairman Mao. She was among three hundred other young delegates. It was in the Great Hall of the People. The crowd lined up in five rows on an expansive terrace. In the background hung an embroidered landscape of the Great Wall. She was in the middle, two heads away from Chairman Mao. They had stood waiting for him for three hours. When he finally arrived all the delegates screamed in tearful joy. She told herself not to blink when the cameraman called for the shot. This was the picture of her life and she didn't want to ruin it. But the more she wanted to control her blinking, the worse it got. Then the camera shutter clicked and it was over. Now she had a picture with the nation's greatest savior, her eyes half open and half shut — in the middle of blinking.

• • •

I wandered the streets for hours trying to come up with a plan to save Evergreen without destroying Wild Ginger. I felt crushed by a great weight. I bumped into bicycles. At one point I became lost. Finally I had an idea. It was the only thing I could think of.

I decided to turn myself in.

I decided to confess to being a co-conspirator, to "share" Evergreen's crime in hope that his sentence would be reconsidered and reduced. I had no idea whether or not the plan would work. But I knew for sure that without Evergreen, my life would not be worth living. At this point, the idea of being in jail meant being closer to Evergreen. On another level, I see now, I also felt a need to punish myself — for not being able to turn Wild Ginger in.

I dared not speak to my family about my plan. It would be more than shame and pain I would bring them. I was sure that my parents and siblings would try to talk me out of it. I was a coward but I was in love. I loved Evergreen and Wild Ginger, and I couldn't bring myself to give up either one of them.

I was eating my last meal with my family. Eight of us sat around the table under the bare lightbulb that hung down from the ceiling. We ate salted bean curd with porridge. We were all quiet for a while. Then my sisters and brothers began to talk about Evergreen's sentence.

"It was too heavy," said my sister.

"Too heavy?" my father sneered. "In 1957, your seventh uncle was sentenced to twenty years in jail just because he was a policeman before the Liberation. They said that he served the wrong government. Thank heaven that other family members were not dragged in and thrown into jail or forced into exile. That could have happened; it is an old tradition brought down from ancient rulers."

"The government doesn't need a reason to put anyone in jail or shoot them these days," Mother sighed. "I wonder why Evergreen did what he did. Maple, do you have any idea?"

"Mama, he didn't do it."

"But he was caught, wasn't he?" my brother said. "The tools were found in his bag."

I tried to control my tongue.

"Was it a trap?" My sister turned to me.

"Who did it?" my brother pressed.

Everyone's chopsticks stopped moving and all eyes turned to me. I buried my nose in the bowl and sealed my lips.

"You weren't involved in any way, were you?" asked my sister.

I shook my head.

"Was it . . . Oh, I am afraid of my own thoughts." Mother put her hands over her mouth. "Wild Ginger is a good kid, although she has tried to play rough. I am sure it was only to show her loyalty to the party and earn political credit. She is not an evil kid, but . . . What do I, an old lady, know about today's kids and their minds? Misery and sadness don't necessarily breed an angel."

Father put down his chopsticks and turned to me.

I got up before Father had a chance to order me to tell the truth. I made up an excuse, saying that I had to attend a Mao study session at school, and dashed out.

The next morning I got up early. I went to the city hall and asked to see the head of investigation. After I told them that I was an anti-Maoist and had been involved in the incident I was led to an interrogation room.

An armed man appeared. He introduced himself as Mr. Wang, an assistant to the investigator. "The party and the people are glad that you have come to your senses. Welcome back to Chairman Mao's line." He told me that I had to produce a written confession before the investigator would see me. "You will have one week to draft a statement."

"Do I write it here?" I asked.

"That's right."

"May I go home at night?"

"No."

"But . . ."

"I am sure you have prepared yourself for a hard journey."

"Well, do I get any credit for turning myself in?"

"Who do you think you are? A heroine?" He turned around and slammed the door behind him.

I was put in a room without windows. I began to compose my confession. I didn't have much to say except that I had supplied Evergreen with the pliers and the bag. To weave a lie was not as easy as I thought. If I didn't make myself compelling, my plan would fail. If I said too much, I would expose Wild Ginger. I decided to simply call myself an anti-Maoist and write abstract words around that label.

It sounded stupid. But what else could I possibly produce? The trick was to make up facts and stretch logic. For example, we all believed that we could endure atom bombs. The fact was that we had no idea what an atom bomb could do. Chairman Mao had said that we needn't be afraid. So there was no reason to be afraid. And we weren't. We were told that if we dug deep enough into the earth, we could generate an earthquake in America. We had no doubt about that. How could Chairman Mao be wrong?

It was the easiest thing to arrest an anti-Maoist and blame the country's misfortune on him. People relished making discoveries. And people enjoyed putting villains in prison. Without learning the bad luck of the others, how could one realize one's own good fortune? An elderly lady in our district was convicted because of her anti-Mao crime. Her cat ate up her lard and she chased the cat out of the kitchen and into the lane. She shouted, "Kill the cat! Kill the cat!" She forgot that the word for cat *(mao)* sounded the same as the Chairman's name. It was too late when she realized her mistake. She should have shouted, "Kill the one whom mice fear!" Another anti-Maoist was an old man. He had stomach problems and farted during a Mao reading. When he refused to publicly criticize himself, he was sent to a forced labor collective for the rest of his life. In contrast, there was a young boy who was considered a hero because he cried "A long, long life to Chairman Mao!" when he drowned in a flood.

I could no longer make sense out of life.

There had been no sign that my case would be brought to light. I was given a bowl of water and two buns every day. I had turned in my papers and was told to wait for a response. I became frustrated as the days went by without any news. I began to realize that I had done the dumbest thing in my life. I was cold at night lying on the bare floor. A plastic container served as a chamber pot. It had no lid. I breathed my own waste. I banged on the door on the tenth day and asked to speak to the investigator. The guard came and said that my food of the day would be taken away as punishment.

After two months of isolation my wait ended. Mr. Wang came and read me the news from a yellow paper. He read in a slurred, impatient, and careless voice, as if he had been reading this all his life and was sick of going through it again.

I learned that my fake confession would have no effect on Evergreen's case. I was sentenced to life in prison as an anti-Maoist.

"The sentence will be effective immediately after a public rally." Mr. Wang threw me the paper and walked off with his hands locked behind him and a cigarette between his fingers.

. . .

I had killed a hen in trying to fetch an egg. I was foolish. But I did what I had to. The prosecutors didn't even bother to interrogate Evergreen to check whether I had told the truth. Maybe they did check and Evergreen had respected my wish. Maybe, who knows, Evergreen knew the truth. Otherwise why didn't he claim his innocence? Maybe he wanted to protect Wild Ginger. Maybe he understood her jealousy and felt guilty about his betrayal. By remaining silent he compensated for her loss.

Anyway I was the fruit of victory for the prosecutors. Now they could go to the general party secretary and be rewarded as heroes. There would be promotions and medal-giving ceremonies. The secretary could be confident that the party's face had been saved. The masses would be warned and the lessons learned. This had always been the purpose of public executions.

I wondered about Wild Ginger. I wanted to know her feelings before I was locked away from the sunshine for good, and before the prosecutor put a bullet in Evergreen's head. I needed to hear Wild Ginger's thoughts on the show she had originated.

I didn't hate her. I hated myself for pushing Evergreen to attend the singing rally.

I now realized that it was the old Wild Ginger I had been trying to reach. The irony was, at least it seemed, that when it came to my choice of whom to rescue, Wild Ginger was the only one on my list. I was still amazed at the fact that I didn't turn in Wild Ginger in exchange for Evergreen's life. What drove me? With whom was I in love?

I couldn't hear my heart's answer. Yet I did what my heart bade me. What was the confusion? Was it because Evergreen was not mine to begin with? Was it always in the back of my head that he was her lover? Was it my fear? Was it the doubt that I could never make Evergreen mine which stopped me from loving him fully? Or was it something else? Something completely opposite. Something like, if I took Evergreen away from Wild Ginger then might she focus her attention on me? For the first time I began to wonder, Was I in love with Wild Ginger? How else could I explain my sacrificing Evergreen to her safety? Was it easier to convince myself that Evergreen had never been able to stop loving Wild Ginger? Was it the fact that Wild Ginger and Evergreen continued to love each other that hurt me, hurt me so deeply that I had to destroy Evergreen and myself?

24

I spent my eighteenth birthday in jail. I had
no regrets. At eighteen I had long been trained to extinguish regret. To die for a cause was glorious. We were
brought up on the farewell letters of the revolutionaries.
Jiang Jie, Hui Dai-ying, and Sheng Bao-ying, to name a famous few. I began to prepare myself, to serve my sentence
like a war captive. I began to accept the fact that Evergreen would be shot and I would spend the rest of my life
mourning the loss. It could have been worse. It seemed
better to remain in jail than to face Wild Ginger and the
question of why I had concealed the murderer of my lover.
Prison had become an escape. To avoid seeing Wild Ginger
was to avoid the stain of my memory.

I was aware that my mind was going. The nut that
wouldn't crack was "Life will mean nothing after I lose
Evergreen." Still, I couldn't help picturing the two of us
spending our lives together up in the mountains, in a poor
village, struggling gladly to provide children a glimpse of

light. The thought never failed to bring tears to my eyes.

I remembered a story from One-Eye Grandpa. He said he'd once had a hard time explaining to a group of village children what a book was. They had never seen one. He was a veteran at that time and was passing through the town. I was sure Evergreen and I would have made a difference. What a pity.

Strangely, I missed Wild Ginger. I often mentally relived our childhood. I had plenty of time. I enacted on my mind's stage events at the school gate, the classroom, the seafood market, the "zoo" dances, and the closet. I forbade myself to think of Wild Ginger as a Maoist. The image of her speaking through an electric loudspeaker distressed me. I chose to fill my mind with her songs in French. I treated my memory with care. I was bidding goodbye to both of my lovers as they had lived and was saying hello to their spirits. In the process I felt a weight lift from me.

It was at that point, in the middle of my mind's flight, she appeared. "The investigator," a guard announced.

Wild Ginger emerged from the shadow and entered my cell. She stood by the door and didn't move for a long time. She was observing me. She was in her uniform and her hair was tucked neatly inside the cap. She had a new watch on her wrist. My heart sped up. Somehow I had been expecting her. I stood up, not to welcome her, but to acknowledge her presence.

"Leave us alone," she ordered the guards. They exited quietly and closed the door behind them. The echo of their steps came, then faded. Deadly silence. We could hear the sound of our own breathing.

She had changed a great deal, I observed. She looked exhausted. The light in her eyes was gone. What was left was a drab day. I was used to her unruly style, so her silence made me feel odd. I began to think of something to say to break the silence. Our time together was gold. Maybe I should ask her about my family. Maybe I should ask her to protect them with her power. I wanted her to deliver a message to my mother, to say that I did this for love — I had promised to marry Evergreen and it was a wife's duty to go into exile to be with her husband. Yet I found it hard to speak these words.

She sat still on one side of the bench. The bare bulb shone between us, blanching our skin. She glanced at the door as if to make sure that the guards were not listening. Then she turned to look at me and waited for me to talk.

I still couldn't open my mouth. A moment ago my thoughts raced, but now I had none. I stared at her fists resting on the table. They were the same fists that had punched Hot Pepper to protect me — a fleeting thought that zipped through my mind's sky. I swallowed a mouthful of saliva.

As if in response to my staring she withdrew her hands. She took off her red-star cap and placed it on the table. Her lips moved but nothing was uttered. I couldn't help thinking that this was the last time I would see her. I tried to stop my sorrow from welling up. Little by little, my mind began its final drawing. The features in front of me that I loved. The thin eyebrows, the almond eyes with yellow pupils, the long and delicate nose. The mouth, which could have such an unyielding expression. It felt unbearable to continue looking.

"Maple, you know it was me." Her lips finally cracked. "You know it was a setup." Her voice was low and husky. "Why didn't you tell?"

I tried to suck some air into my lungs and then shook my head.

She looked at her watch. "Speak." Her breath was heavy.

"The damage is already done. Someone has to pay the price," I said. "Someone has to be punished. If it is not Evergreen and me, it will be you."

Her eyes looked down and she bit her lower lip and held it.

"I made up my mind, that's all." I felt relieved to be able to say this to her.

Her lips trembled and her tears began to come. She tried hard to press back her emotion.

"I wish you well, Wild Ginger," I managed to say. "For what we had, for what you have done for me in the past, for what . . . I have done that hurt you — although I am not apologizing."

Abruptly she got up. Without saying another word she pulled the door open and exited.

I sat with her cap in front of me. Suddenly I was hit by a dreadful pain. It ground my stomach. My hands reached out for the cap.

25

October 1, National Independence Day. My name was called. As I walked through the prison hallway I was silently stared at by prisoners behind bars. In their eyes I saw pity and fear. Returning their gaze, I could hear the screams inside their heads. Suddenly I thought I should sing like the heroines in Madame Mao's revolutionary operas, the women who face death with the kind of calm that suggests they're merely going home. But my teeth were chattering and my tongue stiff. I could hardly walk straight.

With my hands tightly bound I was pushed onto a truck packed with convicts. As the gate clashed closed the truck took off. I didn't know how long the journey would be. We passed open fields, mountain areas. I was in tears when I saw cows grazing on the hills and tall corn waiting to be harvested. None of my fellow passengers were looking at what I saw. Their faces were soil colored and their heads were slumped between their knees.

In the afternoon the road became smooth. There was more traffic and I recognized that we were in Shanghai. The sunlight streaked through trees onto the pavement. It was the annual celebration time, and this was the day to "kill the hen to scare the monkeys." I never thought that I would be the hen. The pedestrians showed no interest as our truck drove by. A few children followed the truck and shouted, "The villains! The villains!"

The men walked with expressionless faces, all in Mao jackets. The women carried their baskets and dragged their children. They walked fast. I longed to find my mother or father among them. I was sure that my mother had been looking for me. She probably had had numerous fights with the authorities already. My siblings had surely made the rounds of the correction houses. I knew the little ones would. They would walk miles to the Number One Shanghai Prison and sit on the edge of the pavement across from the house for hours on end. They would watch the guards changing shifts and inspect the trucks transporting convicts, hoping to get a glimpse of me. They would sit till dark, without food, without water, as I once did waiting for my father at the district's labor collective office. It was the place from which he had departed. I knew that he wouldn't be there. But I missed him so much that it made me feel better that I was waiting for him.

I knew what awaited me. Year after year, I had witnessed so many men and women escorted by soldiers to the rallies at the People's Square. Their heads were shaved.

When I was little I didn't doubt that they were villains. I was always happy to see them executed. I shouted slogans and threw rocks when their trucks passed through the streets. The city authorities loved to display the "revolutionary fruits." Twenty-three years ago when Chairman Mao's Liberation Army took over the cities they paraded through the same streets. Their "fruits" included U.S. tanks and other weapons. Today the convicts were roped like New Year's presents.

When the driver made a stop at a brick building without a sign and a number, more prisoners clambered on, including one I immediately recognized as Evergreen. It had been months since I had seen him. His head was shaved to the scalp. His features seemed hardened. He looked prepared. If I hadn't been roped, I would have thrown myself at him. He gave me a weak grin as our eyes met. There was no bitterness in his expression. I supposed that he too had chosen to sacrifice himself. I admired his determination but was jealous that he let himself be punished for Wild Ginger.

We arrived at the People's Square. As the truck cut through the oceanlike crowds, the young people were chanting Mao quotations. "'The reactionaries are hostile to our state. They don't like the dictatorship of the proletariat. Whenever there is an opportunity, they will stir up trouble and attempt to overthrow the Communist party and restore old China. As between the proletarian and the bourgeois roads, as between the socialist and the capitalist roads, these people stubbornly choose to follow the latter.

They are ready to capitulate to imperialism, feudalism, and bureaucratic capitalism. Such people are extremely reactionary . . .'"

I felt spit on my face, then rocks. Someone got hold of my hair and wouldn't let go. The truck kept going. With a terrible tearing pain a patch of my hair was yanked off along with a part of my scalp. The crowd cheered. They shouted, "Down with the anti-Maoist!" I was enraged, but I couldn't move, couldn't wipe off the blood dripping down my face. I spat back at a youthful face. She ran over, clinging to the slow-moving truck. I felt her fingernails plowing through the skin on my face.

The crowd began to sing. It was one of my favorite songs — the Mao poem "Capture Nanking." "'Rain and a windstorm rage blue and yellow over the Bell Mountain, as a million peerless troops cross the Great River. The peak is a coiled dragon, the city a crouching tiger more dazzling than before. The sky is spinning and the earth upside down. We are elated yet we must use our courage to chase the hopeless enemy . . .'"

Suddenly I doubted my motivation. Maybe it wasn't as sacred as I thought. Maybe all I was doing was trying to beg for Evergreen's love. Look at me, I am willing to sacrifice my life for you. I am better than Wild Ginger. See for your own eyes. Look, Evergreen, here is the one who is willing to go all the way, to die for you, and there is the other who has ordered a bullet in your head.

The truck moved through the sea of red flags and ban-

197

ners. At every jerky stop I moved myself toward Evergreen. Finally, our shoulders touched. We looked at each other and I saw sorrow in his eyes.

The rally had begun. The People's Square was a small-scale Tiananmen Square. Since there was no Gate of Heavenly Peace, the bleak, flat-roofed, Russian-style city hall was the tallest structure in view. It was heavily decorated for the celebration with red flags and banners draped from every wall. A crowd of hundreds of thousands gathered around a makeshift stage and shouted, "We owe our life to the Communist party! We owe our happiness to Chairman Mao!"

I was pushed off the truck with the rest of the convicts. We were escorted to a dark room inside the city hall. I smelled shit. Several convicts had already lost control of their bowels. Others started screaming and making incomprehensible sounds.

Trying to shut them up the guards struck them with the butts of their guns. It didn't stop them. The guards pushed the convicts toward the stage when their names were called. Every time when the door toward the stage opened, the wavelike sound of slogan shouting hit our faces.

I began to look for Wild Ginger. My mind spun. Suddenly I couldn't accept this, couldn't allow Wild Ginger to murder Evergreen and imprison me. I needed to break my silence. I could taste the regret in my mouth. For the first time, I thought, Wild Ginger is not worth it.

"Wild Ginger! Wild Ginger!" I screamed. The guards

came and kicked me. I rolled on the ground but kept screaming.

Wild Ginger wasn't hosting the rally. I assumed that she would appear later as an important speaker. She once told me that Chairman Mao always spoke last at meetings.

Evergreen's name was called. As the guards pushed him toward the stage he turned to look at me. I sensed that he was bidding me a final goodbye. "Maple, I'll come back a tree." He was in tears but he was smiling. "I'll keep your life green. If you ever get out, please visit my grandmother on Bei Mountain. She is ninety-three years old and lives in a temple on top of the mountain. It's called the Cliff Temple. Tell her to watch out for a cricket singing under her bed at every full moon. Give all my Mao buttons and books to Wild Ginger. Tell her that I was a proud anti-Maoist."

He was in a bloodstained white shirt and blue pants. In a few minutes he would be a martyr. I broke down.

"Down with the anti-Maoists!" The shouting came from the loudspeaker. "Down! Down! Down!"

I was already in hell. I saw a reason to destroy the world, the world in which Wild Ginger would go on living as a celebrated Maoist, and would feel no repentance. My conscience rebelled against my heart. My mind gathered its courage. My eyes sought the microphone and my voice prepared itself. The speech was already composed in my head. I knew exactly what I was going to say. I was going to say that I was sick of pretending. Then I would spit out the truth. The whole truth, starting with the closet and ending with the backstage conversation.

I gave myself permission to break the promise, to declare that my love for Wild Ginger was over.

"Convict Maple" was called through the microphone. The guards' clawlike hands came and grabbed my shoulders. They locked me in their grip and pushed me toward the stage. They lined me up with Evergreen.

I pivoted my head toward Evergreen. His eyes were closed and his chin protruded toward the sky. His face was a mask of sadness.

I stared at the microphone. I felt my legs shaking. My chest quaked.

A man with tiny eyes and fat cheeks appeared before me. He had a pair of scissors and an electric shaver. The guard pulled my arms behind my back and tied them there. I was pushed to my knees. Suddenly the sky was draped with the folds of skin under the fat man's chin. He started to shave my head.

The crowd boiled. It looked like a million termites.

My hair dropped in bunches. I thought of a hen being plucked in the market.

I told myself to wait for my moment to address the crowd.

Suddenly someone else's name was called. I was lifted from my knees and shoved down the stage.

I was exiting. No! I realized that I would not be given

a chance to expose the truth. How foolish I was! The reason some convicts were given a moment to speak was because they couldn't talk — their vocal cords had been removed!

Despair overwhelmed me. I kicked and struggled with all my might. The guard hit my newly shorn head with the back of his gun.

The trucks were parked on the side of the square. It was loading time again. The guards pushed Evergreen toward the first truck while I was led to the second. I broke the guards' hold and threw myself at Evergreen. I yelled his name hysterically. I fell on the ground. Four other guards came trying to quiet me. But I was wild and desperate. I held Evergreen's leg. My tears wet the bottom of his trousers. It was too late. Nothing was going to save him. I had come to my senses too late. I had helped Wild Ginger murder him.

Where was Wild Ginger? *The heart remains pure if the eyes don't see,* my dead grandmother's voice said to me. How smart of her to hide now. But I was certain that she was somewhere watching us. Her mind's eye saw every second of this. She counted the minutes left for Evergreen to breathe and the time left for me to be warmed by the sun. Had I been wrong all the way back to the day we met? Was there ever a Wild Ginger who deserved a place in my final thoughts?

The guards stepped on my wrists. A sharp pain shot

through my hand. I let go of Evergreen's trousers. I let go of my love and my life.

It was then that I heard a voice. Her voice. Far away but recognizable. I was sure it was she. She was talking through a loudspeaker. From high above. From the flat roof of the city hall.

My head turned, and with it a million other heads. The focus sharpened, toward a tiny figure standing on top of the roof waving madly, holding a microphone. Behind her, the setting sun looked like a giant red lantern.

The voice sounded distorted. The syllables came broken, as if cut by a gust of wind. "Long live Chairman Mao! I am the Maoist Wild Ginger. Stop the execution! Chairman Mao teaches us, 'A true Communist is a person who is noble, selfless, and lives for the cause of building Communism and to sacrifice herself for the people!' Well, I contradicted Mao's teaching! I am here because I can't explain what's happened to me. I deeply apologize to Chairman Mao. I am ashamed that I had to choose a coward's way . . . If I can't be noble, can't be selfless, can't live for the cause of building Communism, I can climb on the altar . . ." The figure moved along the edge of the roof as if looking for a spot to jump. In one moment I envisioned her fall. My breath skipped.

"But I am too low for Chairman Mao. My sacrifice would not be acceptable for him. My blood has bourgeois ink in it. I am not fit for the revolutionary altar . . . I am a waste, what can I tell you? I'll die and the significance of my death will weigh less than a feather. But I am not going to cry. At least I will act like a Maoist, so you will know I am not a fake. At the core I am who I've always claimed to be . . . My friend Maple was stupid. She was not a Maoist. She needs to be reformed. She's a thief who stole hearts. But the singing rally incident had nothing to do with her, neither with Comrade Evergreen . . . I am here to tell you the truth. I am a Maoist. I do what I have to do because I practice our great leader's teaching!"

She moved to the corner of the building and shouted, "Chairman Mao teaches us, 'Many things may become baggage, may become encumbrances, if we cling to them blindly and uncritically. Let us take some illustrations. Having made mistakes, you may feel that, come what may, you are saddled with them and so become dispirited; if you have not made mistakes, you may feel that you are free from error and so become conceited. Lack of achievement in work may breed pessimism and depression, while achievement may breed pride and arrogance. A comrade with a short record of struggle may shirk responsibility on this account, while a veteran may become opinionated because of his long record of struggle . . .'"

"What is she talking about?" voices yelled from the crowd.

"She is going mad!" the guard escorting Evergreen uttered in amazement.

"She is mad!" the crowd cried.

"Wild Ginger has gone mad!" The crowd stirred.

"Somebody do something!"

"She's going to jump off the building!"

"No! Wild Ginger, don't do it!"

The crowd surged toward her like an ocean tide.

"Be still!" Wild Ginger called from above. "I want you all to listen carefully! I am a Maoist alive or dead. But I had impure thoughts. I tried to resolve my personal grudge but it backfired. I dishonored Chairman Mao, and I must punish myself for it. But please" — she bent her knee slightly — "remember me as a Maoist! A Maoist! A Maoist!"

She leapt.

26

I saw Evergreen free himself from the guards and lunge toward where Wild Ginger lay. The guards swarmed over him as if he were attempting an escape. "Get an ambulance!" Evergreen yelled. "An ambulance! Somebody!"

"For heaven's sake, her skull is crushed," an old voice came. "She'll be lucky if death finds her; otherwise she'll live only as a vegetable."

The crowd resumed its beelike sound.

The microphone buzzed.

I felt stifled and gasped desperately for air. I wanted to move but my limbs wouldn't cooperate. Tripping over my own steps, I fell again and again. My forehead knocked on the concrete.

I crawled my way through until I was beside Wild Ginger. She lay motionless. Her face was pale purple. Her eyes were shut and her lips clamped tightly. No more Mao reciting. The blood was spreading from the back of her skull. Her hair covered half her face. She was in her uniform, washed and buttoned.

Her hands were still warm. I took them.

The sea inside my head started moaning. My world became white, like the negative of a photo.

Slowly her blood came, soaking my trousers.

Hot Pepper emerged from the crowd. She rushed to Wild Ginger and began to search her pockets. Before she went further a policeman stopped her. He searched Wild Ginger's pockets himself and took out a blood-soaked envelope.

27

I don't remember how I got back to the cell. When I woke, I found myself lying on the bare concrete. It was chilly but I was sweating and running a high fever, slipping in and out of consciousness. I kept hearing my mother's voice. "Maple, go and take a look; Wild Ginger is calling you." I felt detached from my body. I couldn't lift my fingers or move my toes. My head spun threads of memory. Still unable to move, I started to recite Mao quotations uncontrollably. "'Communism is a complete system of proletarian ideology and a new social system. It is full of youth and vitality; it is the most complete, progressive, revolutionary, and rational system in human history. It is sweeping the world with the momentum of avalanche and the force of a thunderbolt . . .'"

The image of Wild Ginger jumping off the building repeated itself in front of my eyes. Her leap was like a child's acrobatics, like hopping off a fig tree. I could hear her laughter. Also Evergreen's. I kept seeing their faces. They came to me like the moon's reflection in the water. When I woke, the reflection broke. And when I fell asleep it was a new moon again. I could hear the sound of the water, splashing the stone edge of the pond. I remember the moment I turned to look at Evergreen. In the sound of *Long live Chairman Mao!* his smile froze. It was a hideous expression, like a person who gets his head chopped off in the middle of telling a joke.

In my faintness the guard came. "Get up and say long life to Chairman Mao!" When I raised myself up he came to unlock my cuffs. "Get out, you are free." He cleared his throat and spat his phlegm on the ground.

I asked what was going on; he replied, "How would I know?"

At the prison office I received an explanation.

Wild Ginger had admitted her guilt in the letter. She confessed that she and Hot Pepper were responsible for the singing rally incident. However, Hot Pepper denied the accusation. She claimed to be Wild Ginger's victim.

"What about Evergreen?" I was so overwhelmed that I choked. "He was on his way to be executed when the letter was finally read!"

"He's alive. He is a very lucky man. Once again this proves Chairman Mao's teaching, 'Our party will never mistreat a good comrade,'" the officer said expressionlessly. "Comrade Evergreen was rescued at the last minute. It is another victory of the revolution."

• • •

Lying in bed at Evergreen's house we wept. We tried to celebrate our new lives but it was impossible. Wild Ginger was constantly on our minds. Our bodies were locked so much in the pain of missing her that they became immune to desire. We looked at each other, but all we saw was Wild Ginger. And we heard her voice too. The passionate reciting of Mao quotations. I held Evergreen. Slowly we drifted into a deep sleep. In my dream Wild Ginger put me back into her closet. Once again I felt her.

Days, weeks, and months passed. Evergreen and I were unable to make love.

My mother told me that on the day Wild Ginger's body was cremated, she had volunteered to collect the ashes. Against the authorities order, she took the ashes and secretly went to a temple in the mountains. She prayed for Wild Ginger's soul to be at peace and burned incense. She mixed the incense with Wild Ginger's ashes and left the remains in a monastery under an altered name suggested by the head priest. Instead of "Wild Ginger" she wrote "Land Found." She gave me the address of the monastery.

Evergreen left Shanghai. He went to fulfill his dream of becoming a village teacher. I remained behind. We had decided to give up the relationship. We hadn't been able to make it work no matter how hard we tried. There was not much to say. We couldn't mention Wild Ginger and yet we couldn't stop mentioning her either. She died taking a big part of us with her. Every night I could smell the earth's mold and every morning its fragrance.

I didn't go to the train station to bid Evergreen farewell. He didn't ask me. It was as if we both were trying to forget ourselves before we were able to forget Wild Ginger.

I was assigned to work as a clerk at Shanghai Number Thirteen Department Store. I sold pencils, notebooks, and school bags. Once in a while when there was a clearance sale I would think about buying something to send to Evergreen. But I never did buy anything. I didn't have his address. He never wrote. At any rate, I wouldn't contact him even if I had his address.

28

Over the years, I had other men in my life. I dated the ones who knew nothing of my past. Yet I often felt emptiness. I guess subconsciously I longed to unearth the part of myself that I had buried the day Wild Ginger died. None of the relationships I pursued were consummated. There were a couple of failed engagements. I was twenty-nine years old. I felt ninety-two.

My mother died of uterine cancer in 1981. One of her last wishes was to have me visit the temple annually to light incense for Wild Ginger. "We owe Mrs. Pei that," she said. My father never said anything. Released from forced labor camp after seventeen years, he had turned into a man of very few words. He hated the ex-Maoists.

My family members were spread all over the country. Most of them were married and had children. Two of my brothers had become railway workers and one served in the army as a radio technician. My younger sisters were working too. One was a nurse and the other the head of a remote labor collective. We gathered in Shanghai every New Year's Eve. While the children played hide-and-seek under the table, my siblings began to crack jokes about the Cultural Revolution. They joked about Mao, his followers, and the ex-Maoists. The tone was cynical. I was never much of a participant. To me, the Cultural Revolution was a religion, and Wild Ginger was its embodiment.

This year at the New Year's Eve table my father toasted me with heavy rice wine. He said forgetting was the best way to be happy.

After the fireworks I went to visit the house at the end of Chia Chia Lane. It had been turned into a storehouse for preserved vegetables. It belonged to the market. All the Mao murals, paintings, and calligraphy of Mao quotations and poems around the neighborhood had been scraped and coated over with layers of cement. There was no trace of Wild Ginger except the fig tree. Its trunk was bucket thick now and it bore a tremendous amount of fruit in the summer.

I made my first visit to the temple on the fourth day of the spring. The temple was located in the midst of the mountains. The climbing was difficult. The Buddha's statue sat within a large cave. Behind the statue was a monastery where Wild Ginger's ashes were kept in a tiny ash drawer by the altar, which was covered with red silk fabric; in front of it hundreds of candles were burning.

Not until then did I understand my mother's intention. It was her way to help me to come to terms with my loss and sorrow. She knew that I could never forget Wild Ginger and Evergreen. She knew that I had to reconcile with them in order to go on with my life. Mother had waited patiently for my enlightenment.

The walls surrounding the altar were covered with quotations copied from Buddhist scriptures. In essence, they seemed to be about moving and floating through life without stopping and without letting bitterness get in the way. Was I bitter?

It had been almost nine years since Wild Ginger's death. The country had pulled down its mask after Mao. Being an ex-Maoist brought one embarrassment. The Cultural Revolution was officially criticized as madness and destruction although Mao was not yet questioned for his responsibility. In the neighbors' mouths, the incident at the Mao quotation-singing rally was a sad story. No one remembered Wild Ginger as a heroine, only as a foolish girl.

It was big news in the paper that the Russian-style city hall was scheduled to be demolished on October 1, the National Independence Day. A new hotel that had Japanese investment backing was to take its place. The year was 1994, twenty years after Wild Ginger's jump.

I felt distracted that morning. The city hall was in front of my mind's eye. I was eating breakfast when I heard the announcement from the radio in the cafeteria where I worked that the explosion would take place at nine o'clock. I found myself imagining the explosion. I had an urge to be a witness. The feeling became so strong that I had to excuse myself. I left work without permission. Taking a bus, I headed to the People's Square.

Afraid that my remorse would be unbearable I had avoided this place for years. And I had been right. My memory was as fresh as yesterday. My tears flowed the moment I stepped off the bus. The sight of the building brought Wild Ginger right back to me. I could see her speaking to me vividly. "Maple, don't ever feel sorry for me. I take the wounds as medals!" But I also heard her laughter. The sound of silver beads dropping on a jade plate. I was able to admit to myself that I had been lonely for her all these years. There was not one person who could understand and share my feelings.

Suddenly I missed Evergreen terribly.

I felt weak. My mind kept unleashing itself. Was he a village teacher? Did he ever miss Wild Ginger? Or me? Was he married? Who would she be? A village girl? His student? Or another woman, another village teacher who taught at his school?

A worker at the square told me that the explosion would take place in five minutes. "It's an old ugly building. It no longer carries significance. We have brought down a lot of the same kind in Beijing. It's interesting that not many people have bothered to come to see the spectacle. When I was doing one in Beijing, the crowd was —"

Suddenly I saw what I took to be an illusion. A man of Evergreen's figure walked into my view. I blinked my eyes and shook my head. The image was still there, still moving. My hands went to cover my mouth. I dared not breathe; it seemed that if I did I would break the illusion, as a drop of water would chase away the reflection of the moon in the pond.

I stood, stared, unable to move.

This is not a mistake, I heard my mind say. It's him.

The worker turned toward the man. "Hey, you! Step out! It's too dangerous! Get out! You hear me? Out! This way! Hurry up!"

The man turned toward us, smiling apologetically, and suddenly he saw me. His smile froze and he stopped in his tracks.

The worker went and pushed him out of the area.

29

From his features I learned how I had aged. He was a real peasant with deep gaplike wrinkles and weatherbeaten skin. He wore a washed-out green army coat and a pair of worn boots. He was covered with dust. Yet he was solid.

For a moment we were awkward. Words halted our tongues.

The loudspeaker was giving the last warning about safety. And then came the countdown.

Both Evergreen and I turned to look at the city hall. I was sure he saw exactly what I saw.

Like a piece of silk fabric Wild Ginger fell from the building, descending in slow motion.

My mind leapt backward. I saw her sixteen-year-old face.

"You know what, Maple? I am burning fire, the heat itself. Nobody can extinguish my passion for Chairman Mao.

I feel so happy and complete. It is Chairman Mao who saved me from withering and kindled my spirit into a glorious blaze!"

Through my tears I felt Evergreen's hand. He came to hold me. I felt his breath on my neck.

I turned to him. There was no hesitation in his eyes. He was determined to pursue what he was doing. His eyes were asking for my permission. I wanted to tell him that I had been waiting for him all along. I wanted to tell him that I was ready. I tried hard to push, to get the words out.

He sealed my words with his lips.

I closed my eyes.

The sound of explosion came.

I tasted her in my mouth.